ROBERT S MURILLO

THE THIRTY-THIRD FLOOR

Five Short Stories

2015

Orinda, California

The Thirty-Third Floor

Robert S Murillo

Copyright© 2009, 2013, 2014 and 2015

www.robertsmurillo.com

AUTHOR'S NOTE

Since publishing *The Vanity* three years ago, I've been locked in my Dungeon, working on my first volume of short stories. Today, the creaking door has opened and I'm pleased to announce the completion of *The Thirty-Third Floor.* Within its covers are five strange and intriguing tales about five brokers who work at the esteemed firm of First Fargo Securities located on the thirty-third floor of the famous Bank of America Building in San Francisco.

I also have been working on *The Make-up Room*, the follow-up novel to *The Vanity. The Make-up Room* is a tense cross-time adventure set in 1941 and 2014 that pits an eighteen year-old Veronica Lake—along with our hero Mike Lundy from *The Vanity*—against unstoppable time *and* the powerful Axis powers. It should be available by late spring 2016.

I want to thank a few folks that helped make *The Thirty-Third Floor* a reality. First, to my wonderful wife, Suzanne—proofreader and critic par excellence. To Mark Hooper, my Barcelona editor for putting all the pieces together. Also to my bud in Ashland, Chris Honoré, for his insights and encouragement. And to good friend and inspiration, Darryl Brock.

I believe *The Thirty-Third Floor* will amuse and entertain you—and may even provide you with some insights into the world of finance. Paperback and Kindle versions are available on **Amazon.com**. If you have questions or comments regarding the stories, please email me at **robert.s.murillo@gmail.com.**

My website — **www.robertsmurillo.com** — is under construction but you will be able to see some of the other projects I am working on—and the works that I have completed.

For now, I hope you enjoy *The Thirty-Third Floor*.

—*Robert S Murillo*

For my Sue, who has no clue how to get from
Point A to Point B without
Going first to Point C… and D… and E…

Contents

VILLA ZARRI

Brad Fisher was considered by his buddies at First Fargo Securities to be "The Thirty-Year-Old Virgin." A gifted workaholic, Brad spent all his days—and most nights—focused on building his business. Making cold calls. Asking for referrals. Gathering assets. Doing research. His silent response to his comrades' teasing was simply his impressive success. But his social life? Unless one defines a meeting with a prospect or client as a "social" event, he had none. Every day was just another workday for Brad Fisher.

Until today.

Brad stepped off the elevator as the doors slid open on the thirty-third floor. He checked his watch—it was exactly seven o'clock. He nodded to Jessica, the receptionist, and marched down the hallway, entering his office. He had a busy morning planned and was anxious to start.

"What's this?" he said aloud, finding a vertical package wrapped in plain brown paper on his desk. "Bottle of wine?" His first thought was that it was from Kevin, his manager—a little perk he provided to those brokers who surpassed their previous month's gross. Brad peeled away the paper, expecting a nice California vintage, but to his surprise, he found a bottle of *Villa Zarri* Brandy Italiano. The bottle was tall and narrow; the brandy, amber and pure.

"What the hell…?" He held it up, admiring the label.

Hanging around its neck, a black string held a small, folded card. He removed it and looked inside. Handwritten, the note read, "*Never sin alone.*"

Brad smiled, impressed with the marketing ploy but puzzled by the card's message. It usually read something like "*Congrats on another outstanding month!*" Or "*Keep up the good work!*" And it had always been signed by his manager.

"Maybe a client brought it by?"

He called Jessica.

"No, Brad, nobody dropped off anything for you this morning. Unless they came before six."

He hung up. "Gotta be Kevin," he said to himself.

But as Brad slipped the bottle into his attaché case, he hesitated. "Wait a sec. I didn't beat last month's numbers."

Later that day, the bottle of *Villa Zarri* long forgotten, Brad drove across the Golden Gate Bridge for an afternoon appointment in Tiburon with his client, Lisa Gibson. It was a convenient way to finish his day since he lived in nearby Mill Valley.

Lisa was a valued account. She'd inherited a tidy sum from her parents, who'd died in an auto accident while on a trip to Mendocino to celebrate their 30th wedding anniversary. Brad had managed their accounts and now helped Lisa with her investments. She was twenty-eight, pretty in a girl-next-door way, and she lived alone.

The two of them sat on the leather sofa with Brad's attaché case before them on the coffee table. He snapped it open to remove the folder containing her portfolio and saw the forgotten bottle of brandy. So did Lisa.

"And what do we have *here*?" Lisa asked. Without waiting for an answer, she reached for the bottle, held it up and said, "*Villa Zarri*? Never heard of it. Is this stuff any good?"

"No clue. Found it on my desk this morning."

"Let's try it!"

"But…"

"Oh, loosen up, Brad!"

"I really shouldn't…"

"The client is always right. Now, pour!"

"We'll probably won't even like…"

"Oh, for god's sake, open it!"

A half-hour later, Brad was in Lisa's kitchen pouring the second round of *Villa Zarri*. He'd shared his theory of the brandy's mysterious appearance and shown her the provocative note that was attached, maintaining the whole thing was just some stunt perpetrated by a few brokers in the office. "I can't imagine a *client* dropping off such a gift with a note like that."

Lisa read the note again. "*Never sin alone.*" She looked

3

up, smiling. "Someone obviously knows you pretty well." She slipped the string along her ring finger. "One thing for sure." She held out her hand, admiring the hanging note. "Your mysterious 'benefactor' has excellent taste. The brandy's *very* good."

Though Brad Fisher felt the warmth of the *Villa Zarri*, he attempted to maintain his faculties.

After all!

Still, he found himself humming *"That's Amore"* while measuring out another inch and a half of the tantalizing, tawny drink in the short, wide tumblers. He even held them up, closing one eye, checking to make sure they were even. With tightened lips and a nodding chin, he approved of his work.

"Perfect!"

Meanwhile, Lisa had made herself comfortable on the overstuffed couch that faced toward the kitchen, paging through her last month's First Fargo statement. She unwittingly fanned herself with her free hand.

"These statements drive me crazy! I can't tell what I paid for anything! Or when I bought it! And where does it show my insurance policy? Do you guys do this on purpose?"

Brad grinned. "I'll be right there, Lisa. I'll walk you through it *again*; it's really not that difficult," he teased.

"Don't patronize me, *Mister* Fisher!"

Brad set the glasses down on the kitchen counter, picking up the cork stopper and slowly inserting it snuggly into the bottle. A few drops of the brandy dribbled onto his fingers. He licked off the pungent and tasty liquor as he peered through the small opening between the bottom of the kitchen cabinets and the countertop, taking in a slice of Lisa. He watched her hands as she flipped through the statement laying on her lap, he saw her knees, and a little more.

Lisa Gibson had been divorced for two years. Fortunately, there had been no kids. Her story wasn't uncommon: Ken—the ex—had wandered from home one too many nights until reason and dignity finally won out over hope and patience and Lisa locked the door. That there were tears wasn't a secret, but she stood her ground, and time, that Great Healer of all wounds, had eventually salved her heartbreak and disappointment. The mention of Ken's name no longer stabbed at her or brought her grief. In fact, knowledge that he had married and been divorced again had, for some depraved reason, provided Lisa with an indescribably delicious satisfaction.

Brad and Lisa's relationship had always been platonic. They'd once attempted a brief good-bye hug, but it looked more like each was embracing a freshly painted mailbox. No handshakes, no high-fives. Discussions—generally brief between them—were mostly on business, the stock market, and, of course, the poorly devised First Fargo statements.

"Sooo… where is this 'second coming' of the *Villa Zarri*?" Lisa said sarcastically, without looking up. She wiped her brow with the back of her hand.

"It comes!" he replied, somewhat dramatically, sweeping out of the kitchen, turning the corner, tumblers in each hand, brandy sloshing.

"Now, what don't you understand?"

He offered her the glass in his left hand. She looked up, reaching for drink with her right hand. She was about to respond about the puzzling and frustrating format when her fingertips brushed the tops of Brad's fingers. Instantly, she sensed the soft texture of his skin, the warmth that emanated from his body, his nearness.

A jolt of electricity lit her from within. Her heart rate shot up, and there was a gentle throb and slight moistening between her legs. An inner voice shouted, *"Oh my God!"* Her eyes went round, and her face, already flush, appeared to combine surprise and delight and fear in one expression. In a low uncontrollable — almost guttural — murmur she moaned, "Ooh… *Ooh!*"

The First Fargo statement slid to the floor as she reached for the lapels of Brad's tweed coat.

By some miracle, he was just able to place the drinks on the coffee table before she yanked him down on top of her. She groaned, closed her eyes and moved her hips against his.

Brad hesitated, but only for a moment. He was soon attacking her neck, her face, her ears with lips and tongue while fumbling with the buttons on the back of her blouse. Frustrated, he yanked apart the silky top, sending the stubborn buttons flying. She grabbed at his hair and pushed him down to her breasts as she arched her back…

"Wow! This is *some* brandy, this *Villa Zarri*."

"We were warned." Brad grinned. "And I'm sorry… I mean about your blouse and all."

"Am I covered?" she said, peeking over the edge of her glass.

Brad looked long at Lisa. "Well, right *now*, no." He took her glass and set it on the coffee table next to his. "But I'll check your policy in the morning."

EVERLY MANNINGTON

*Here begins a treatise how the high
Deity sends his messenger to summon one creature to
come and give account of his life in this world.*

"It's over!"

"Whataya mean 'It's over'?"

Tears ran down Jessica's cheeks as she forced herself to look straight at the man she loved. "Just that. It's over."

"But why? What did I do?"

"I knew I shouldn't have gotten involved with you. It's just, I thought..." Her words faded into sobs. She blew her nose.

"What do you need? Is it money?"

"Money?" She let out a disappointed sigh. "Oh, Everly, you just don't get it, do you?" She looked toward the elevators nearby. "Look, I have to go. I need to be at the front desk by six." She pulled out a fresh tissue, wiped her cheeks and got up to leave.

He grabbed her arm and looked up at her. "Meet me here, at Peet's, at ten. Promise me."

She bit her lower lip, hesitated, nodded, and then ran

off toward the elevators. He waited until she was gone, then walked to the same bank of elevators and rose to the same floor.

Everly Mannington stepped out onto the thirty-third floor of the building now known as 555 California Street but still more popularly referred to as the "B of A Building." The whole floor belonged to the prestigious firm of First Fargo Securities, where its dimly lit lobby and hallways with brass trim and dark green carpeting reeked of excess and money.

Everly, who most days would have walked directly to the receptionist and laid a long stem rose on her desk, instead walked right by and proceeded directly to his office.

He stabbed the ON button with his index finger on his Krups Espresseria machine located on the credenza along the wall, then turned and walked to his massive, L-shaped desk and switched on his computer. Immediately, his oversized HD monitor lit up. While the espresso machine spit and gurgled Peet's famous Arabian Mocha-Java into a small porcelain cup, Everly Mannington strolled to his window, not even noticing how the rising sun to his right was illuminating the Golden Gate Bridge and Marin County's picturesque hills above Sausalito.

"What's with Jessica?" he whispered.

As the Espresseria spattered its last drop, signaling that his 'hot shot' was ready, he walked back to the coffeemaker, picked up the cup, took a sip of the dark brew, and let out a satisfying 'Aaah' sound. He turned, leaned back against the credenza.

"Why would she say 'it's over'?" He weighed the worst-case scenario, the consequences, assessing the pros and cons as if it were an investment in a stock. Finally, he said to himself, "Whatever. I'll take care of it when I see her at ten." He set the cup down and checked himself in a mirror hung behind his door. He ran his fingers through his hair and straightened his tie.

Everly was what many folks would describe as the quintessential *stockbroker*. He was tall and trim, and good-looking enough to turn a head. He wore tailored Armani suits, Dolce & Gabbana dress shirts and Brioni silk ties. He was charismatic — yet not necessarily in a positive way, assuming an air of confidence that bordered on cocky. And though there were some in the office who generally *wanted* to like him, they found it difficult. Others plain tried not to — and found it easy. But Everly Mannington didn't care what they thought. At twenty-eight, he was one of the largest producers at First Fargo and enjoyed the perks and the lifestyle that went with that success.

As he did each morning, Everly scanned the pinkish *Financial Times* and the *Wall Street Journal* searching for any useful or pertinent news and marked a few items. At 6:30 sharp, the U.S. security markets would open and trading would begin — providing another day where many an investor's dreams either came true or were soundly dashed. The truth of the matter—though he *wanted* his clients to be successful—Everly made money on stock trades whether his clients made a profit or not. They were the casino players; he was the 'house.'

And the house was on a roll. Last week, he'd gotten a 'thumbs-up' on a $45,000,000 account with Sterling Research, a rapidly growing biotech company near San Jose that was anxious to go public. And, on a tip from a so-called 'insider,' Everly had recently invested $50,000 of his own money in a small 'start-up' company—CGI (Computer Graphic, Inc.)—at a dollar and half a share that had closed yesterday at three sixty. He'd also convinced one of his more aggressive clients to jump in at the same time for the same amount. And lastly, Everly Mannington, despite his arrogance and his narcissism, had found himself in love with Jessica Brooks, the company's receptionist.

Jessica spent most of her morning dispatching incoming calls to the brokers. Though overqualified for this kind of menial work, Jessica had jumped at the opportunity to work full-time at First Fargo after temping there for two months. Its location was ideal, providing her the centrality she needed in her search for a position as a graphic designer—a profession where she could make use of her education and her natural talents. But, for now, particularly with the recent recession swelling San Francisco's unemployment rate, she was thankful she'd secured this job.

She was blessed with kind, blue eyes, a lithe, healthy body, skin most women dreamed about, and a warm smile that invited smiles in return. Her twenty-fourth birthday was this Saturday. Her plans? Well, she knew what she *wasn't* going to do: spend it with Everly Mannington! Not after the conversation she'd had with him this morning.

Everly closed the *Journal* and was about to check to see where his penny stock would open when the phone rang.

"Everly, this is Kevin."

"Kevin! Hey, bro, how goes it?" It was his manager. Not many managers would tolerate being addressed as 'bro' by a broker, but when a broker was producing almost $2.5 million a year during a recession, there were certain concessions a manager would make. However, this time, there was no 'concession' in Kevin's voice. "We need to talk, Everly. *Right now!*"

"Sure, let me grab a fresh cup of espresso, and I'll be right over." He hung up the phone. Was there a tinge of 'something's wrong' in Kevin's voice? He grinned it off, set the machine at ES (Extra Strong), then checked his monitor to see if the market had opened yet—it hadn't. He grabbed the small cup of hot, pungent coffee, and strolled over to his manager's office, walking right in.

"What's up, Kev?" he quipped.

Kevin looked up and said flatly, "Close the door and sit down."

Everly Mannington closed the door, sat down, crossed his legs, flicked a piece of lint off his pants, took a sip from the white porcelain cup and flashed his even whiter teeth.

"Everly, I have some bad news. I just received a call from Compliance. That penny stock you bought last week for your account—CGI—was not blue-skied in California. Not only that, our Compliance people have found that the company was a shell; some of the so-called founders have been arrested and the stock was de-listed this morning. It's worthless and obviously won't open today."

"Whoa! Are you telling me my fifty thousand is gone? There's no way of getting any of that money back?"

"Most likely not. And that may not be the worst of it. You're forgetting that the stock wasn't blue-skied. As a 'stockholder' *and* a financial advisor, you'll be subject to questioning and a possible fine." He paused. "I'm not sure what I can do about your blue-sky blunder, but I can assure you that you'll be receiving a phone call from our Compliance people in New York. And don't mess with them, Everly. Just answer their questions."

Everly Mannington slowly walked back to his office—some of his bravado missing—mumbling to himself.

"Fifty grand. Gonzo!"

He entered his office and sat down. His voicemail light was blinking. He picked up the receiver and punched in his voicemail code. Immediately a metallic male voice politely informed him that he'd had one call at 6:34 that morning. Then he heard an anxious, "Everly, this is Ian. Where are you? We need to talk. Right away!"

Everly Mannington slowly hung up the phone. Ian Spencer was his partner in the Sterling deal and was handling the IPO side of the offering—the stock distribution, the tombstone, the timing.

"Great! What's with Ian?"

He made another cup of Peet's best espresso and wandered over to his window again. In spite of his personal loss in the market and now a possible issue with Ian, his thoughts drifted back to Jessica and the special birthday weekend he'd planned for her in Carmel—*and* a proposal that included an engagement ring with one round-cut 2.63-carat diamond, which was securely locked in the glove box of his car downstairs...

Suddenly, Ian burst into his office and blurted, "You should return my calls! We got problems, my man!"

Everly Mannington internally winced and thought, *What's going on?* But to Ian he simply said, "What's up, Ian?"

"I just got a call from a buddy at Merrill. Seems like some hotshot in his office has been giving tennis lessons—and who knows what else—to ol' Sterling's daughter. And now the word is 'Daddy Dear' wants to 're-think' the deal with us. I don't like the looks of this, Everly."

"I'll call him. The old guy and I hit it off really well when I was down there last week. We'll be fine. Not to worry."

But Ian Spencer *was* worried. "Call him this morning, for God's sake! Call him now! I've already spent most of the money I thought we'd bagged."

Everly, annoyed by his partner's haughty, presumptuous attitude, retorted, "*Look*, Ian, I said I'd call him. Have I ever failed before?"

"But…"

"Relax. I've *got* this guy. I've put together a sweet deal for him, and he has no reason to walk. He's mine. You know me. It's *The Art of War*, my friend. And I'm good at it."

"Yeah, yeah…" But Ian knew Everly was right. Everly *was* good at 'it.'

"Look, go spend your money. Sterling Research is a done deal."

"But…"

"Look, I *said* I'd take care of it. Now, if you don't mind, I've got things to do. I'll call you as soon as I know anything."

With a sound reminiscent of a pig snort, Ian marched out of Everly Mannington's office.

Everly smiled. Though still early, he knew Dr. Sterling would be in, aware that both men shared in the 'early-bird' theory. He picked up the phone and dialed the office of Sterling Research, asking to speak with its founder and president, Dr. Richard Sterling. He thought he'd be placed right through as he always had been. Instead, he was placed on hold for more than two minutes before he heard, "Dr. Sterling is in conference right now. You might try calling back later."

Might? Try? He didn't like the sound of that. Last week, he'd spent most of the day with Sterling. They'd played golf in the morning, had lunch, and then, over coffee, had laid the groundwork for a possible public offering early next year. Sterling had been excited about the future, delighted with First Fargo's credentials, and elated with Everly Mannington. Now Sterling was seemingly ignoring him.

Everly tried every half-hour for the next three hours. Finally, he was told that Mr. Sterling would not be available for the rest of the day.

"…but if you wish to call back tomorrow?"

Everly slowly slid the receiver into the cradle. "What the *fuck* is going on?" He scornfully looked to the ceiling — and beyond — for an answer.

Everly Mannington took a deep breath and let it out slowly. He checked his Rolex. Five to ten. He grabbed his coat and hustled to the elevator. It dropped thirty-three floors, letting him out in the lobby. He saw Jessica sitting at a small round table in front of Peet's. She saw him but didn't wave. He smoothly slipped into a chair across from her right on time.

"Hey, Jess. What a morning! You wouldn't believe…" He stopped. He could see her eyes were still red, her face, flush. "So what's up? Talk to me." She remained silent. "You're not serious, are you? I mean about us being through?"

Jessica stared at him, tears welling over again until both cheeks were streaked again. Her hands remained in her lap, clutching multiple tissues. She was unable to speak.

"Damn it! What is it, Jess?" He went to reach for hands that weren't there.

Jessica took a deep breath. "Ev… I saw my doctor yesterday," she said bravely, evenly, blotting her eyes; she tried to fake a smile, gave it up, and sat up straight. Then she leaned toward him—her voice mostly a raw whisper—and said, "She says I may…" Her voice faded so that just Everly heard.

"*What?*"

Everly Mannington made his way back to his office, collapsing heavily into his chair. He leaned forward, placed his elbows on the desk, rubbed his forehead with the tips of his fingers and let out a long sigh.

He slowly looked up and saw that his voicemail light was blinking again.

"What *now*?" he cried as he punched in his code. It was Kevin.

"Where the hell have you been? Compliance called looking for you, and they're not happy. You didn't mention that you solicited—and bought—this CGI shit for a client here in California without filing and providing the *Important Information on Penny Stocks* statement that *you know* your client must read, sign, and deliver before making any purchases. You bought this guy twenty thousand shares! At almost two bucks a share! You're going to have to personally cover that, Everly. What were you thinking? Get your ass over here as soon as you get this message! We need to call New York back immediately!"

This time, when Everly Mannington left his manager's office, he was visibly shaken. Compliance had been relentless, uncompromising, and unsympathetic. Everly's shoulders sagged, and he dragged his feet across the thick carpet until he found his office. The last thing Kevin told him was, "Get out of here for the rest of the day! We'll talk more about this tomorrow!"

Everly grabbed his coat, flipped off the computer and the espresso machine, and stood for a moment trying to recover his poise—the 'cool' that he'd always personified. He walked by Ian's office without looking in. Fortunately for Everly—or maybe for Ian—Ian was on the phone, looking out his window.

As Everly approached the elevator, he saw that Jessica wasn't at the front desk; Stephanie, a sales assistant, was still covering for her.

"You be back, Everly?" Stephanie asked.

"No… Tell Jess…" he paused. "Never mind."

The elevator 'binged' and the doors opened. It was empty.

He took the elevator straight down to the

underground parking garage, stepped out and, gathering himself, stood tall. In spite of his morning from hell, Everly Mannington kept his fury and frustration bottled up. He inhaled, holding the air for a moment before slowly exhaling. Some composure regained, he pulled back his shoulders and almost strutted to his car.

Maybe I'll take a drive across the Bridge… cruise the headlands… Assess the damage…

He hit the button on his key fob to open the car doors and immediately heard the double beep, seeing the amber taillights blink. But when Everly Mannington got to his car—a black Mercedes SL63 AMG Roadster—he froze. The left side mirror was dangling from the door by its internal parts and wires. The door itself had been attacked by someone wielding a sharp object—probably a key—that had left deep, multiple gashes in the paint. The driver's side window was shattered. He ran to the opening, looked in and saw that the glove compartment door had been forced open.

"Shit!"

He threw open the driver's door and slid into the car, sitting on hundreds of tiny pieces of glass, and leaned toward the glove box. He reached in and felt around. *The ring was gone!*

The color drained from his face and he gripped the steering wheel until his knuckles turned white. His eyes, round and distant, slowly looked up through the windshield. On the concrete wall in front of his car, a sign read: "PARK AT YOUR OWN RISK!" It might as well have said "THE LAST STRAW!"

Everly Mannington's mind, the mind that could see through every obstacle in packaging a lucrative business deal, "the mind that could bind" the different personalities of a many-sided and complex proposal— now quietly 'snapped.' Instead of yelling, pounding the dash with his fist, or seeking the managers of the parking lot, he slammed the car door shut, the hanging mirror banging heavily against the damaged side of the car door.

He started the powerful engine and threw the gearshift into reverse. The sports car literally jumped out of its parking place, scraping the side of the Cadillac Escalade parked in the next stall. He hit the brakes, shoved the shift lever back into drive and floored the accelerator pedal, laying rubber and fishtailing through the underground lot.

When he got to the pay booth, he slowed just enough to be able to crash through the wooden guardrail and still make the sharp right-hand turn up the exit ramp. Again, he pushed the accelerator to the floor and literally left the building airborne.

He landed solidly, barely missing a cable car full of tourists heading westward up California Street. The cable car's bell clanged and the passengers screamed, but Everly heard nothing. He aimed his car eastward but, to avoid ramming a bike messenger, swerved right onto Montgomery Street and sped toward Pine.

Jessica had remained at Peet's.

What am I going to do?

As she wiped away another flow of tears, she noticed a few folks at the nearby tables staring at her.

Got to get out of here.

She grabbed her purse and, realizing she was out of Kleenex, decided to walk down to the drugstore. She exited the building onto Pine Street, turned left and was greeted with a bay breeze that felt refreshing on her flush cheeks. She crossed at the corner and entered the Walgreen's located on the northeast corner of Pine and Montgomery where she bought—and opened—a small package of Kleenex. She pulled out a tissue as she exited, blew her nose, and strolled the few steps back to the corner to wait for the light to change. She removed another tissue to blot at her cheeks and became frustrated by the length of time the light was taking.

Come on!

As if waiting for her command, the red WAIT turned to green WALK, and Jessica Brooks stepped off the curb and into the intersection.

His eyes afire, his car rapidly approaching the corner of Montgomery and Pine, Everly was suddenly aware of a young woman before him crossing the street growing larger and larger. She turned to see Everly's car racing toward her, her eyes now enormous, her face a mask of terror. She screamed...

Everly hit the brakes, crying out, "Noooo!"

~~~~~~

"Everly, Everly, you're so impetuous! *Take it easy.*" The voice came from a man calmly sitting in the passenger seat. He was well dressed, at least a generation older than Everly, and undaunted by the circumstances. He sipped on a lid-covered Venti extra-hot chai latté from Starbucks and let out a self-pleasing "Aaah… *perfecto!*"

Everly's Mercedes had stopped and time had ceased outside the vehicle.

Everly looked at the man, then out his windshield at Jessica, who was a few feet in front of his car, as still as a figure from Madame Tussauds—and a nanosecond from death. Everly quickly turned back to his passenger.

"What the… What the *hell* is going on? Who are you? Is she okay?"

Everly's passenger—who looked a bit like Kevin Spacey—nodded. "Of course, Everly. Everything's fine. *For now.*"

"How the hell is this happening?" Everly spun around, peering out all the windows, taking in the area that now embraced him: everything was frozen in time—his world, a tableau. He swung back to his visitor, noting that they were dressed identically, down to the same tie. "Who the fuck are you? What's going

23

on? Start talking, buddy, or I'm going to…"

"*Calm* down, Everly. And *such* language!" He took another sip of his latté and patted at the corners of his mouth with a napkin. "Look, I'm just a broker like you. Or is it an account executive? I always thought 'financial advisor' was a bit pretentious, didn't you? He sipped again, savoring his drink. "That's a *darn* good drink!" He removed a spec from his lapel.

Everly glared.

"Yes, yes. Who am I? You can call me 'Piper.' Good solid name—*Piper*. I have other names if you're interested."

"*God damn it!* You know what I mean…" Everly leaned toward the man.

Piper recoiled, turned away and whispered toward the passenger window, "No, he didn't mean it. …No, no. I'll be okay."

He turned back to Everly. "Listen. It's all quite simple. Within the next few seconds, Jessica here will end up on Market Street." He was referring to San Francisco's main thoroughfare three blocks south of where they were.

"That is unless we can put together a trade or a deal—you know, 'something for something?'"

"What are talking about? 'Something' for what?"

"As I said, Everly, I'm just a broker like you. Except, I'm not offering stocks or bonds." Piper paused for effect. "You see, what I do is remind folks that success in life, well, that it isn't necessarily free. That there's more to success than just hard work, dedication, and material things. And so, when they realize this, we're able to come to some sort of an 'agreement.'"

"Agreement? What kind…?"

"Ah ah, Everly!" Piper said, holding up his index finger. "Let me finish." He took a sip of his chai latte, turned toward Everly, and in a deeper, throatier voice, said, "Then, there are those who want *more* – who believe that enough is no longer enough. They climb over their fellow workers, step on their friends, and they forget their families."

"What the *hell* are you talking about? I haven't…"

"Everly, Everly, you've wandered. You were such a fine young man. Remember when you were ten years old and you spotted those oily rags that had caught fire near your neighbor's house? How you ran, possibly endangering yourself, and put the flames out. That house would have burned to the ground! And the time you saved your younger brother when he overdosed on pain pills after he'd failed the bar exam? You practically carried him to the ER on your back. Now, he's a prosperous lawyer down in San Diego. And he has two kids – one named after you! You were an Eagle Scout and captain of the soccer team at State. The list of your good deeds goes on, Everly. You weren't like this until you started working at First Fargo."

Piper went to set his coffee in the cup holder but decided against it. "Am I correct?"

Everly stared at the man called Piper.

"Everly, you've changed. Your road to this new lifestyle has been at the expense of so many—but mostly to yourself."

"I've never done…"

"Denial! Don't play games with me, Everly." Piper turned to face Everly squarely. "You're a borderline crook! All that stuff about *The Art of War*! Don't try to kid me!" he said, decibels rising.

"What are you talking about? I haven't…"

"Oh, but you have, Everly. You have. Recall a few years back when you were just starting out. You wanted success so bad. There were a half dozen or so brokers at First Fargo who wore those expensive suits, drove sporty cars, and lived the life of Lotharios. You wanted to be like them. And though you envied them, you wished them misfortune. It was your goal to be number one, no matter what it took.

"And your desire has come true, hasn't it? You have 'taken' accounts from your companions, oversold products rich in commissions, and 'traded' some clients' accounts that really needed no adjustments. As a result, you've alienated yourself from most of the other brokers."

"Not true. I've done…"

"How about the Robinson account? They didn't need those ETFs to replace their bonds. Not that some ETFs are so bad. But you suggested the switch, sold their bonds, and collected a few extra basis points. And for buying the ETFs, you received a nice, fat commission.

And let's not forget the Baldwins from Oregon. You sold them the 'A' share mutual funds with a hefty front-end load when the 'C' shares with no load would have sufficed for them. Even the Sterling deal wasn't yours originally. You managed to rip that off from a rookie you were supposed to be mentoring! Need I go on, Everly? There are other examples—most occurring under the radar, of course. Most, management missed—or they looked the other way. Sadly, they just see the impressive numbers you're racking up."

"Nobody's gotten hurt…"

Piper cut him off again. "And then along came Miss Brooks."

They both turned to look at Jessica through the windshield, standing there, staring at Everly, her eyes wide, unbelieving, her face full of horror, knowing death was an instant away.

"I imagine you love this woman. And such a pretty lass, too. She's been the best thing that's happened to you since you became a broker. Deep inside, you know that, Everly. And that mammoth ring you got her! Wow! Nice show of your love. Or of your money? And I bet you'd like to have it back, right? And what about that stock—CGI? Wouldn't it be nice to know the company's legit and the stock *is* 'blue-skied' in California? Oh, and how 'bout a nice, friendly phone call from Dr. Sterling?"

"How in *hell* do you know about all these things?"

"Aaah, those words, 'in hell.' Believe me, I've dealt

with some individuals with one foot already in Satan's palace. Done some of my greatest work with them, my boy." Piper turned to Everly, his face aglow. "Listen, we're both businessmen. You need a little help. No, I'd say you need *a lot* of help. And, right now, I'm seeking something from you. Though, I'm not sure you understand what I…"

"What the… Wait a minute! I got it. This is like that classic story… What's it called? Where what's-his-name sells his soul to Satan." Everly laughed.

"Aaah, a man with a literary background. I like that!" Piper took a nip of his latté, stared out the windshield, hesitated and then answered deadpan, "Not exactly."

"Except you're gonna fix all these so-called bad things that have happened today… if I turn my soul over to you. Right?"

"Yes, but… not exactly."

"You set me up in a position to kill Jess then want my soul as a bargaining chip to save her."

"Aah, not exactly."

"*Quit* saying that! And anyway, that's *not* a deal. That's blackmail!"

Smiling now, Piper said, "Not exactly, Everly. I was hoping you might realize just what you're doing…"

But Everly Mannington cut *him* off now. "Look, Piper, or whatever your damn name is, I'm thinking…" and Everly swept his hand a hundred eighty degrees in front of him, "…how do I know *any* of this is real? In fact, it can't be real! Hell, I'm thinking if I say 'no' to you, and I hit Jessica, get arrested, thrown in jail, I just might wake up in my bed, all of this having been a great, big nightmare!" Everly, feeling his confidence building, now turned up his decibels and added, "How about you take your little blackmail act and stick it *exactly* up your ass?"

"Everly, please! You've got it wrong—*dead* wrong. You want to think this is a dream, that's fine. But I can assure you, *you ain't dreaming!* Pinch yourself, Everly." Piper's voice took on a deeper, more somber note. "Listen carefully. I wiggle my nose, and your life continues on its current course. Jessica ends up on Market Street, and you go to jail. *And* you'll have *no* memory of me. In fact, you'll end up in San Quentin, where, I hear, there are some inmates who'd take great pleasure in a nice young lad like yourself. Know what I mean?"

Piper paused, looked at his coffee cup, his chai latté mostly gone now, and mumbled something about wishing he'd also gotten a slice of the angel food cake.

Finally, Everly stated, "I'm *not* selling my soul!"

"You're just *not* listening, Everly; I *never* asked to *buy* your soul. And this isn't Goethe's *Faust*; I'm *not* granting wishes in exchange for your soul. Nor am I Satan, come to take your possessions like in the biblical story of *Job*. On the other hand, you may want to consider the classic tale about those folks who have become so absorbed in material wealth that they've forgotten to appreciate all that has been given them."

"I do *appreciate* what I have!"

"You're *still* missing the point, Everly. When was the last time you cared about something—or somebody—other than yourself?" Piper waited, staring at Everly. "U-huh. Didn't think so."

"How else does one acquire…" Everly stopped. Then said, "…success."

"I know one thing: success is not something that comes by manipulating those around you, Everly. *Your* so-called success has come because you've submitted to Temptation, Everly. Excess and Envy stand sentinel at your office door. You're not successful. You're a failure. No one likes you, no one respects you. What's happened to you this morning is a friendly reminder of many things which have become important to you."

Everly turned to Piper. "'*Friendly* reminder?' You've destroyed me! I have little, if anything, left!"

"Think, Everly! I haven't destroyed you. Like I said, I'm only trying to make you *aware*." Piper took a small sip of his chai latté, then looked at the cup, disappointed that it was nearly empty. "Like this cup, Everly, the good deeds in your personal book of accounts appear depleted."

Everly wanted to react but could no longer find the words.

"Your only worthy achievement since arriving at First Fargo has been getting Jessica to somehow fall in love with you." Piper paused and turned toward Everly. "Then—and I can't believe you did this—when she needed you the most, what did you do? You offered her *money*!" Piper winced. "Look out that window, Everly. *Look!*"

Everly stared at Jessica. She remained unmoving, petrified, yet a tear had streaked down her cheek.

Piper swirled around the remains of his drink, then finished it, bottoms-up. "Tasty!" Once again, he tapped the corners of his mouth with his napkin. "Think of me as the brother who saved you from an overdose of ego and greed."

Everly gripped the steering wheel until his knuckles went white, knowing Piper was right.

Piper smiled. "Well, that's it! I really got to get going." He dusted off his pants and said, "By the way, I hear the views of San Francisco Bay from San Quentin are quite remarkable—particularly from the showers." He set the empty Starbucks's cup in the cup holder between them and folded his napkin, placing it in his inside suit pocket. "Well, Everly?"

Piper turned and faced the young man. "Time is, as they say, 'up!'"

"What do I need to do?"

"Oh, Everly, you know exactly what to do!"

~~~~~~

He literally marched from the elevator across the lobby where he found Jessica sitting at a small table in front of Peet's. Before she could say "Hi," he handed her a long-stem rose, kissed her on the cheek, and whispered huskily, "Beware the weekend!"

"Everly! What are you *doing*?" She looked about the open area in front of Peet's trying to hold back a grin. He'd never kissed her before at these brief, morning meetings for coffee.

"Something's has happened, Jess."

"I can tell! Does this have to do with the text you sent me this morning? You said you met someone."

"Yes, I did. But, first, tell me. How did things go with your doctor, yesterday?"

"Well," she paused, coyly. "She said I was in great shape!"

"Well, *I* could have told you that!"

She shook her head, feigning embarrassment.

Everly paused, reached across and placed his hand on hers. "Seriously. I'm glad everything is okay."

"Thanks, Ev."

Then Everly looked Jessica straight in the eyes and said, "Now, let me tell you what happened!"

She took a sip of her coffee and leaned toward him. "I'm ready."

"You're not going to believe this. First, you dumped me. Told me it was over. Then, I lost all this money in the market. And the Sterling deal? Lost it to Merrill. Then Kevin got angry with me and sent me home. And then someone broke into my car. I… I was about to kill you! But, then Piper showed up. He stopped time. You were frozen. And…"

"Everly, stop! What*ever* are you talking about? Was this some sort of dream?"

Everly took a breath, pondered a moment. "I'm not sure. It was so real. But when I woke up this morning, it was still *today*. And I felt so different…"

"Slow down, Ev!"

"Anyway, Piper showed me things—things I'd forgotten about. And he showed me what I'd become. Jess, I'm changing my whole approach. Going to talk with Kevin. I've got a brand-new business plan in mind."

"Everly, what's happened to you?"

Her cell phone vibrated. She checked the message and immediately looked disappointed. "I want to hear more, Ev. And definitely more about this Piper fellow but I've got to get upstairs."

"Sorry, sweetie. I know. It's just I'm so…"

"I can tell."

They stood up and went to each other. She moved against him, stood on her toes and whispered in his ear, "Love you." She pulled back but remained close to him with the flat of her hand on his chest. Then, slowly backing away, she noticed his tie, a recent birthday gift. She winked at him and said suggestively, "Nice… tie." With that, she walked quickly across the lobby and entered an empty elevator. She turned and faced outward and smiled at Everly, who was still standing in front of the table at Peet's. She blew him a kiss as she disappeared behind the closing doors.

"Quite a classy lady that Jessica," came a voice from behind him.

Everly spun around and there, sitting at the table, was Piper.

"I knew it! It *was*n't a dream."

"Not *exact*ly," Piper said, mimicking himself.

"There was a Starbucks's coffee cup in my car."

"Speaking of Starbucks, Everly, how's *Peet*'s chai latté?"

"It's excellent." Everly paused, then said, "Scout's honor."

"Well, I guess I'll have to try it, then." Piper got up. "I gotta jump, Everly. Just wanted to remind you to take good care of her." He turned and started for the counter.

"Will I ever see you again?"

Piper, hesitated, looked back at Everly and said, "I hope not."

ACROSS THE WAY

T his night would not be a good one for George Thomas Cole. The day, on the other hand, had been particularly satisfying. His Forty-Niners had pulled victory from the jaws of defeat with a last-second field goal to beat the Ravens 23 to 21 and, to celebrate, he was finishing up a tasty dinner at the Mehfil Indian Cuisine and Bar, feasting on the 'special' that evening—something called *Gosht Rumwala*—a spicy plate of lamb cubes cooked in a base curry with garlic, ginger, onions, and a hint of quality rum. *And*, he'd just received a sweet smile from a timeless beauty—trim and elegant—sitting across the way with a group of her friends. George, regrettably, could only smile back.

Besides, it was Sunday and George, a stockbroker with First Fargo Securities, knew the next five days meant 'early-to-bed, early-to-rise' as the New York Stock Exchange opened at 9:30—6:30 in San Francisco.

He paid the bill, and as he rose to leave, he saw that the woman looked disappointed. She subtly lifted a hand and waved. He hesitated; then, with a shrug, he turned and left.

The cool October night that greeted him felt

refreshing as he literally strutted down Fillmore, feeling a bit inflated about the 'contact' he'd had with the flirtatious lass.

"Pretty lady," he said, grinning.

It was about this time that George's stomach fully realized what he'd consumed at dinner. And his stomach wasn't pleased, sending out a series of gurgling sounds.

…And a great meal, George thought, playfully patting his belly in response.

Arriving at California, he turned right and headed west toward Steiner—homeward bound—when he was stopped in his tracks by a wave of some of the most tantalizing smells on the planet. Across the street, Sift Cupcake and Dessert Parlor called to him like a Greek siren beckoning Odysseus. Usually able to say "No" to Sift's sweet seductions, tonight George was gently lifted off his feet and carried through its front door by the enticing aromas. Before he realized what had happened, he was marching up California, sipping on a large 'Stud Muffin Cake Shake'—a creamy concoction of a brown sugar beer cupcake, salted caramel frosting, and cayenne-dusted bacon blended with milk and ice for the best no-ice-cream shake maybe ever!

He was making loud slurping sounds, sucking every last drop off the bottom of the near quart-sized cup, as he entered his apartment on Steiner, between Pine and California.

"Awesome!" he said out loud, setting down the

empty container.

Wrong! his stomach protested—promptly sending out a series of rumbles sounding much like the thunder from a nearby storm.

Quiet down! George countered.

He then went about preparing his clothes for work the next day and getting himself ready for bed. But, as he turned out the lights to the bathroom, he burped. Up came a nasty swill concocted by his stomach.

Yuk! He swallowed. *Maybe a couple of Alka-Seltzer will right the ship.*

Naaah.

Instead, George slid between the cool sheets of his bed and reached for A. Scott Berg's *Lindberg*—a biography of the famed aviator—a hero of George's. Immediately, George's stomach, let loose a few 'maydays.' Gurgling sounds. Bubbly-like. And more rumbles. But George Thomas Cole—immersed in Berg's tense and dramatic descriptions of the flyer's life—ignored the chaos partying in his stomach and read until after nine-thirty before he began to doze off—the book almost falling out his hand. He marked the page, turned out the light, and closed his eyes.

Gurgle. *Rumble!* A belch sent up another sour smack of curried stomach acid with a hint of curdled brown sugar.

"Gross!" He sat up on one elbow and swallowed. He let a sigh and reluctantly rolled out of bed, went to his medicine cabinet, and found a few outdated square packages of Alka-Seltzer. He ripped a pack open. Plop, plop. He stared at the glass. "Where's the fizz fizz?" Not happy, he swirled the mixture around, drank it, and returned to his bed.

I'll be better in the morning.

Wrong again! His stomach was far from through with him! Within minutes after George had fallen asleep, the stomach's trusty partners—Dreams and Nightmares— surfaced, ready to set loose a bizarre night George would never forget.

George's old Sony digital clock radio clicked over to 5:08, and immediately KCBS's weather report burst into the room.

"…October 19th. Locally, fog will blanket the beaches from Stinson to Santa Cruz. With winds up to 15 miles per hour, temperatures could drop to the low 40s. Expect downtown San Francisco to hit 53 degrees after the morning overcast melts away. Across the bay, Oakland should see a high of 57, while farther inland, temperatures could rise to…"

A hand shot out from a mound of blankets and sheets and slapped the snooze button on top of the radio. Silence returned to the bedroom, but before the radio blasted back on, the covers went flying toward the foot of the bed; George Thomas Cole sat up and flung his feet to the floor. He shook his head, took a moment to scratch, and rolled out of bed.

Forty minutes later, he was aboard the 1 California

trolley—the 1Cal—riding it to Kearny, where he got off and walked the two blocks to The Bank of America Center at 555 California. He picked up a *Chron* and a black coffee at Peet's, stepped into an elevator and zipped up the thirty-three floors to First Fargo Securities. He gave a quick wave to Jessica at the front desk and continued down to his office. He arrived at 6:24 and fell into his chair the same way he collapsed into his sofa at home. He smiled. Not a drop of coffee spilt. He pulled out the Sporting Green from the newspaper and scanned the results of the 49ers game before perusing the business section.

A broker for twelve years—the last three at First Fargo—he loved working here. Prestigious firm, great location, majestic views, successful people, innovative programs. In addition, he loved San Francisco—the unique restaurants, the deep bellow of the fog horns, the clanging of the cable cars, the spectacle of unforgettable sunsets.

George was not into vanity. His suits were off the rack, his dress shirts were 16/35 from shelves at Macy's, his shoes, Johnston & Murphy. Nice, just not overly expensive. He took the trolley to work—didn't even own a car—and currently, there wasn't a woman in his life. For now, the stock market was his darling—his soul mate. He loved the energy, the thrill of the unknown each day. And though 'she' hadn't been particularly good to him lately, George faced his monitor as he always did each morning, ready to play… ready to do battle.

Ready to rumble!

He'd suffered through his worst month in three years last month and was already desperate to find a way to save this one. The Dow Jones had moved down daily, methodically, painfully, mostly due to disappointing earnings from major Dow stocks, problems with the Euro, and troubles in China. Add to that, the Fed's continued cluelessness in finding ways to stimulate the economy, and it wasn't surprising that many of George's clients were sitting tight, with no interest in taking losses, changing their positions, or bringing in new money.

He needed to come up with an idea — something that made sense in this market. Something unusual. Something that would get his clients excited again. But without an idea, George was a ship without a sail. He was down to considering buying a list of leads — an expensive investment that usually yielded only disappointment and at best a write-off. No, he would not buy any lists. Not George Thomas Cole.

List? Lists? I don't need no stinkin' lists!

2

He finished his coffee, debating whether to get another while he scanned the monitor for something that might spark an idea.

"What the…?" he said out loud.

Something wasn't right. There were two stock symbols in the lower right-hand corner of the screen that he hadn't entered, nor did he recognize: HYE and LOE.

"HYE and LOE? Where'd *they* come from?"

And then realizing the inane 'play on words,' he smirked, then laughed, and wondered who'd been in his office, messing with the stocks he'd set up on his monitor. Meanwhile, HYE flashed green, LOE flashed red as HYE nudged up to 33.25 and LOE dropped to 32.75.

"Somebody's got too much time on their hands," he said aloud and leaned forward to delete the symbols. But as he did, he saw that HYE went to 33.30 and LOE dropped to 32.70.

"What the hell? Come on! HYE and LOE? *Gimme a break!*"

He went to delete the symbols again, but as he reached for his mouse, HYE went to 33.35 and LOE dropped another nickel to 32.65. He let go of the mouse, deciding to wait. He got up and walked down to the kitchen for another cup of coffee. Upon returning to his office, he found that his phone was ringing.

It was exactly seven o'clock when he picked up his cordless phone.

HYE was at 34.45 and LOE had fallen to 31.55.

George lowered his voice.

"Cole, here."

"Good morning, Mr. Cole." What came through was a lilting, but well-directed, female voice. "My name is Anne Morrow. I'm assuming the market is open?"

"The market opens at 6:30, Miss Morrow. Can I help you?"

"Oh my! I thought the market opened at seven." She paused. "We need to move quickly, Mr. Cole. I'm calling for a client of yours: D. Whitney Morrow. He's in Mexico on business right now, but he wishes to make a purchase. I realize your firm hasn't heard from Mr. Morrow for a while, but nonetheless, he has some interest in two stocks today. Do you want his account number? And you'll probably need to verify that I have authorization to make the trades for him."

George got up from his chair, turned and casually strolled to his window, looking puzzled. *D. Whitney Morrow? Morrow? The name sounded vaguely familiar. Hmmmm… Must be an inherited account I never followed up on.*

"Yes, sure, Miss Morrow. Hang on."

He was about to turn back toward his desk and check his book for the account when he noticed that the office in the building across the way was occupied. That in itself wasn't strange, even though it had been vacant for the past two months. He was well aware that most offices in San Francisco's Financial District were at a premium and sooner or later, they all got leased out.

No, what *was* strange was the décor. It looked like an office that might have been from a different time. All the furniture was heavy oak, and up against the left wall was a huge, roll-top desk, on top of which stood a candlestick phone and a banker's lamp with a dark green glass shade. Nearby, there was some sort of machine that looked a little like *Star Wars'* famed robot, R2-D2. It was spitting out a thin ribbon of paper. A tall bookcase, containing mostly thick hardback books, rested against the far wall. On that same wall there was a large, colorful travel poster. He could see it read "MEXICO."

In the far corner, a small, metal garbage pail sat like a faithful dog next to a water cooler. To the right, a large, standing fan blew short red streamers parallel with the floor.

The most remarkable sight, however, was sitting at the roll-top desk. For there was a slender, handsome, woman—her long, thin neck creating an impression of aristocracy and elegance. Her dark hair, short and soft, was sculpted into 's'-shaped undulations called "finger waves." From what George could see, it appeared she was wearing a two-piece wool suit. A round, bell-shaped hat sat on the top of the desk. She was on the phone—the receiver pressed firmly against her ear—rapidly tapping a pencil against the side of the phone.

He swore he could hear it.

He stared at her, smitten. Even at the distance between them, he could tell she was striking. "What a beauty!" he whispered—then added, "Someone must be filming a period-piece TV commercial or a movie over there."

"Mr. Cole? Mr. Cole! Are you there?" Anne Morrow's voice shot through George's phone.

He looked at the phone in his hand wondering how it had gotten there. "Oh... sorry. Miss... Morrow, right? Where were we?"

"I asked if you would like the account number. We *do* need to act quickly."

"Oh, yes, of course. The account number. Go ahead, Miss Morrow."

But as George went to turn back toward his desk, the woman across the way looked straight up at him, leaned closer to the mouthpiece of the candlestick phone and said, "It's A261943. The name on the account, again, is D. Whitney Morrow. I'm Mr. Morrow's daughter." She smiled and, with her free hand, waved to him from across the way.

3

George stood there agape.

"Mr. Cole! Are you okay?" she asked, her voice concerned yet melodic and friendly.

George continued to stare at the young woman as if in a stupor. She waved again, smiling, this time more to get his attention. He gave his head a shake and appeared to come out of his trance. But before he could ask what was going on, she said, "Please, Mr. Cole. I need to make these investments *right away.*"

George slowly backed up until he ran into his desk chair. He turned, sat down at his desk, and entered the account number. There was a slight delay, and, suddenly, the account of D. Whitney Morrow flashed up on the screen. There was $500,000 in AAA-rated corporate bonds sitting in a margin account. And he saw that there was a letter on file authorizing Anne Spencer Morrow to trade in the account.

"I... I have the account up Miss Morrow. The authorization letter is still valid. Now what can I do for you?" His voice was now serious, professional, focused — seeking to impress. Still, he was confused by her attire and the décor of the office.

"Mr. Morrow would like to buy 5000 shares of Hydro-Yield Energy at the market. He also wants to *short* 5000 shares of Land Opportunity Enterprises.[1] The purchase shall be done in my father's margin account,

---

[1] *Short selling is simply when you sell a stock that you borrow from your broker — you don't own it — with the promise to deliver the stock back to him at a later date. The proceeds from the sale are credited to your account. At some time in the future, you buy back the stock with the original proceeds and return the shares to the broker. If the price has dropped, you buy them back at a lower price and make a profit on the difference between the proceeds from the original sale and the amount that you paid to buy them back. If the price of the stock has risen and you want to return the stock, then you buy it back at a higher price than you paid and you lose the difference. Make sense?*

Mr. Cole. Do you need the symbols?"

"Yes, if you have them there. What are they?"

"H-Y-E for Hydro-Yield Energy, and L-O-E for Land Opportunity Enterprises."

"What? What did you say?" George sat up straight, turned, and checked his monitor.

"I want you to buy 5000…"

"Yes. I understand, Miss Morrow, but why those stocks?"

"Mr. Cole, I really don't know. Suffice it to say that my father has requested for me to place these orders."

"But…"

"Please, I need for you to act immediately."

George Thomas Cole continued to gape at the lower, right-hand corner of his screen.

What the hell! Hoax? The account exists, the stocks are trading before me, and I see that she has power to trade the account, but…

"Mr. Cole!"

"Yes, yes, Miss Morrow. Sorry. Buy 5000 shares of Hydro-Yield Energy at the market. And short 5000 of Land Opportunity Enterprises. Got it."

He saw that the bonds were marginable up to $1,000,000. And that the purchase of HYE would require about $180,000. He informed Miss Morrow that he needed to put her on hold while he called to find if there were 5000 LOE stock to borrow. Two minutes later, he was back.

"We've got the stock in inventory, Miss Morrow,

though to be honest, I was surprised. Shall I proceed?"

"*Please.*"

"Right away, Miss Morrow." He tapped in the orders, hit 'Enter,' and in mere seconds, the transactions were done.

"Okay, Miss Morrow. Done. 5000 shares of HYE, bought at 34.75 on margin. And you've shorted 5000 shares of LOE at 31.25. Okay?"

"Thank you, Mr. Cole. I'm sure we'll talk tomorrow morning. But *this* time at six-thirty. Will you be in?"

"Yes, but I need your number. We need to talk…"

Anne Morrow had already hung up.

"Wait!"

George sat there. He was not happy. He wanted to know how these stocks had inexplicably appeared on his computer, and how it happened that, soon after, Miss Morrow had called to invest in them. It didn't make sense. Something wasn't right.

He spoke to the phone in his hand. "Damn it, lady, what's going on?" George Thomas Cole slammed the phone down, spun around, and stepped quickly to the window. He looked across the street into her office. From what he could see, nothing was going on.

Except that she was gone.

4

The next day, the scene played out the same. He arrived at work just before the opening bell at six-thirty, this time going directly to his window. She sat at her desk. When she saw him, she waved and smiled—and began dialing. Seconds later, his phone rang and the dialogue was the same.

"Good morning, Mr. Cole. This is Anne Morrow again. Please buy 5000 shares of HYE at the opening. And short 5000 shares of LOE. I will wait."

"Okay, Miss Morrow. But, we need to talk…"

"Please, Mr. Cole, the market is about to open."

"But, I want to…"

"Mr. Cole, please!"

George dutifully performed the trades quickly and competently. But as soon as he confirmed they were done, she promptly thanked him and hung up.

His attempts at "Wait!" or "Hold on, Miss Morrow!" went for naught.

He went to the window. He saw that she'd already put on her coat and cloche. She checked herself in a small mirror that she returned to her handbag, then slipped her arm through the straps of the purse. She hesitated, then turned and walked toward the window; she slowly tilted her head up to look at him. Their eyes locked instantly. There was no longer *any* distance between them. She smiled and went to raise her hand to wave, but suddenly pulled it back. She turned away and marched to the door. She looked about the room, switched off the lights, and left.

"I think she…" He stared at the darkness that filled her workplace. "What the hell is going on? Why is she dressed that way? Why is the room full of old furniture...?" He paused. "I've got to find out... *got* to meet her."

The third day, after placing the same orders, she, once again, hung up on him. Frustrated—and a little hurt—George shuffled to his window. He found her waiting across the way. He looked down at her, wanting her. He tried to smile. Her dark eyes, moist, stared up at him. She lifted her hand. He thought she was about to wave but it was more that she was reaching for him. Then, before he could react, she quickly turned, marched to the door, shut off the light, and disappeared.

"No! No more!" he cried.

On the fourth day, after she'd hung up, he waited while she slipped into her coat and hat. When she appeared at the window, she smiled warmly. He waved back and then George did something odd. He pointed at himself and then pointed downward, repeating the gestures several times. She understood his 'signals' and quickly shook her head and mouthing the words, "No, no!"

But George was no longer there to read her lips.

He'd already dashed to the elevator. He dropped the thirty-three floors to street level, rushed out to Pine Street and waited for her, watching the front doors of the building across the way. *He had her.* She wasn't going to escape!

He waited. And waited. Ten minutes went by. Twenty minutes. A half hour.

"How in the hell...?" Fuming, he returned to his office on the thirty-third floor. He looked down on the unlit office across the way.

"That's it! Tomorrow, Anne Morrow, you and I will meet!"

George smiled smugly. His plan was simple. He would go to her. Tomorrow, she'd be waiting for him to arrive at *his* office but just about that time, he'd be entering *hers*.

5

Meanwhile, George Thomas Cole's business had been thriving. For the past three days, he'd shown the two stocks to most of his 'growth-oriented' clients— clients who weren't necessarily interested in income investments. At first, there was the expected sarcasm and skepticism ("HYE and LOE, are you kidding me?" "Come on George, you're not really serious?" "George, are you prepping for a stint on SNL?"). But George was persistent and, eventually, some of his more speculative clients nibbled. George bought HYE for his own IRA and shorted shares of LOE in his personal account. He got a few friends to go in. Folks had called back after watching it for a day and invested in sizeable positions. And each day, HYE kept its heated pace upward and LOE continued its skid.

He checked his calendar.

Thursday, October 24th. Sam's 1:15. Lunch. David Walker.

David was a long-time client and a good friend. He

too had taken solid positions in buying HYE and shorting LOE. And like many of George's other clients, was pleased with the quick profitable results. By the time the market closed on Thursday, HYE was at 54.50 and LOE was 11.50, and David had gains of over $110,000.

And Mr. D. Whitney Morrow? He had made a half million dollars since Monday.

6

First Fargo Securities had 'business-casual dress' on Fridays, meaning 'neither tips nor ties' were necessary — tips being wing-tip shoes. Slacks, collared shirt, and sport coat were the accepted attire. Understandably, most of the guys in the office participated. Those brokers who did wear the traditional 'uniform' on Friday, were generally those who had meetings with clients that day... and today George had a rendezvous with a very special 'client.'

Suddenly, the old Radio Shack radio clicked over to 5:08 and immediately KCBS's weather report burst into the room.

"...Locally, it should be warmer at the beaches today, temperatures reaching the high 60s from Stinson to Santa Cruz. Expect some mild breezes but nothing more than 3-5 miles an hour. Downtown, the City could reach temperatures in the low 70s. Across the bay..."

A hand shot out from a mound of blankets and sheets and slapped the top of the radio. Silence returned to the bedroom. Suddenly, the covers went flying toward the foot of the bed and George Thomas Cole sat up, tossing his feet to the floor like he did every morning. He shook his head and his stomach gurgled. He didn't feel well. But then, realizing what day it was, he said, "Jesus! Gotta get going!"

George Thomas Cole shaved extra close and applied a very subtle touch of a masculine after-shave. He wore his dark blue suit with a white shirt, silver cufflinks—with GTC engraved on the flat, visible surface—and a navy blue and dark red striped tie. Dark blue socks—plus a cordovan-colored belt with matching wingtips. He looked in the mirror. "Yes!" he said aloud. His stomach rumbled, "No!"

George took two Alka-Seltzer.

Today he was going to her. She'd be waiting for his arrival at *his* office, but he was going to show up at *hers*. To find out about her father's odd investments. To discover the truth about her unusual attire and the dated office décor. And, most importantly, to finally meet Anne Morrow.

He grabbed what was left of an old package of Tums from a drawer in the bathroom and saw there were only two left. *Not good*, he thought. Still, he smiled, excited about his plan to meet Anne. He left his apartment at his usual time—catching the 1Cal trolley near Fillmore at 6:01 AM—which would normally drop him off near Kearney at 6:13. From there, he'd easily be able to walk down to Pine, the street beyond California and The

Bank of America Building, putting him in front of her building at roughly 6:19. He'd be at her office before the market opened.

A little bit about the San Francisco trolley. For all intents and purposes, it's a bus, *but* its operating system is unique. It gets its power from electricity from overhead wires, generally suspended from roadside posts. Rising from the top of each trolley are two spring-loaded trolley poles that connect to these overhead wires, completing an electrical circuit. Power! And the bus moves. One perpetual problem with the trolley, however, are these trolley poles. For a myriad of reasons—from potholes to panic stops—they can come loose from the overhead lines, causing a disconnection. When that happens, the bus stops instantly—becoming literally 'unplugged.' To rectify this inconvenience, the bus carries a special pole rope attached to the rear of the bus, that the driver uses to 'grab' the loose trolley pole, placing it back on the proper electric overhead wire. Once the connection is 're-made,' all is well. Wheels turn. The bus moves.

The 1Cal begins its route at 32nd Avenue and heads east down California, jogging over to Sacramento near Fillmore—where George boards—turns left at Gough, then right on Clay, and proceeds east toward Kearney and beyond. George Thomas Cole, somewhat ashen from swaying from side to side as the trolley wound its way through the commuter traffic, held tightly to the leather strap. He wasn't going to allow his uneasiness to destroy his day.

I'll be fine. His thoughts of finally confronting—and meeting—Anne Morrow were enough to relieve his discomfort for now.

From Fillmore, it was roughly a twelve-minute ride to Kearney. Usually. Normally. But just past Polk, before Larkin, the trolley was forced to quickly veer out of the way of a jaywalker and, in doing so, the right trolley pole sprang loose, immediately breaking the circuit, causing the bus to stop. Lights dimmed and then went out. Passengers groaned, some swearing, some declaring—again—that this was the last time they'd ride one of these 'goddamn antiques.' Behind the 1 California trolley, traffic backed up even farther. The bus driver opened the entry door and stepped out, marching to the rear of the bus. A few minutes passed before he stepped back onto the bus, facing his passengers.

"Folks, we've got a problem. We're a boat without a paddle. Someone forgot to connect the pole rope we use to reattach the trolley poles with the overhead wires. I've reported our little dilemma… but help—this time of the morning—well, is, at least, twenty to thirty minutes away."

A single groan emerged from the packed trolley.

"No!" George cried, realizing that his plan to meet up with Miss Morrow at six-thirty would now be

impossible. His face crinkled with pain. His morning was collapsing around him: a broken-down bus, a riotous stomach, and a failed plan.

And it was just beginning.

A young, well-dressed broker-type, standing nearby, staring at his cell phone, his eyes wide, whispered, "Oh my God!"

George leaned toward the man. "What's up?"

"The stock market. It's crashing worldwide. Looks like a disastrous opening in New York!"

"What!" George wailed. "No! No, it can't be! The Morrow account! All my clients! My personal accounts!" George took off like a halfback, shoving and pushing his way through the exiting passengers, finally finding the rear exit door. He took off down Clay toward Kearny.

"I'll never make it to Miss Morrow's office," he huffed and puffed. "And I'll never make the opening," he gasped. Still, George Thomas Cole ran... and ran...

And ran...

7

He went directly to his office at the B of A Building. It was a quarter to seven. He passed on his usual coffee, did grab a paper, and rushed to the elevators. He popped out at the thirty-third floor, ignored Jessica at the front desk, and jogged to his office.

He flung the newspaper to the far corner of his desk and collapsed in his chair.

Shouldn't have run all that way, he thought. His stomach agreed, making terrible threats. He wiped the sweat that dripped down the side of his face with his sleeve, and checked the market. It was already down over 575 points.

"Jesus!" And his stomach let out a mighty growl.

He swallowed the last two Tums.

A neat stack of pink 'While You Were Out' messages sat next to his phone, placed there by his executive assistant, Phyllis. He quickly went through them, arranging them in some order of importance, then reached for the phone when he realized there was no message from Anne. He went to check the prices of HYE and LOE, hesitated, and, instead, stood up, marching to the window.

He looked across the way toward her office. "What the…" He squeezed his eyes shut and shook his head. When he re-opened his eyes, the view hadn't changed. Lit only by natural light, the office across the way was empty. Not a desk, a lamp, a book, a teletype… or a Miss Morrow. He ran back to his desk to check his screen. HYE and LOE were gone. Two blue-chip stocks occupied the space where they'd been.

He typed in the symbol, HYE. Hit enter. "NO SUCH SECURITY" flashed at the bottom of his screen. Likewise, for LOE.

"This can't be happening…" he said out loud. He ripped off his coat and tossed it in the corner. He continued to sweat. He picked up his stack of messages and went through them again. No references to HYE or LOE. Just, "Call me ASAP!"

Unsure of what to do first, he unconsciously checked his top drawer for some gum.

"Fuck!" He slammed he drawer shut.

He went back to his computer and brought up a cross-reference application that made it easy to find who owned what stocks. He entered HYE, then LOE.

"NO SUCH SECURITY" flashed at the bottom for both entries. Long or short. He went to 'research' and the 'news service.' They too showed no such companies.

He checked the market. It had—at least temporarily—bottomed out and had bounced back. Still down, but now only 425 points, he angrily pushed the messages aside and grabbed his coat from off the floor. He marched out of his office, down the hall, and to the elevators, pushing the button several times.

"I'll be back!" he blurted toward Jessica as he rushed through the opening doors.

Minutes later, he entered the building across the way and made his way to the elevator bank with a group of folks who worked in the building. All of them, most with their coffees, looking fresh and ready for their day, stared at the disheveled George Thomas Cole as they entered an UP elevator. Sweat still streaked down his face, his clothes were wrinkled and damp, his tie crooked and loose. One occupant—hesitant—asked, "Floor?"

He paused. He wasn't sure. "Thirty-two," he finally

said, guessing. Immediately, the small faction looked at each other.

"That's the top floor, mister—it's been closed for the past couple of months," a well-dressed black lady said cautiously. "It's under construction. You... sure you got the right building?"

George, puzzled, remembering there were no floors above Miss Morrow's office, glanced at the floor buttons on the wall. "Sorry, I meant thirty-one." He closed his eyes, leaned back against the wall, placing a hand on his stomach and quietly burped.

"You okay, mister?"

"Yeah, yeah. I'll be fine. Rough morning."

The assemblage seemed to relax though there remained a subtle difference in the distance between him and the rest of the group. The elevator rose, stopping at a myriad of floors, dropping the anxious workers off, the last one on the twenty-eighth floor.

"Have a nice day," an older man said and quickly exited. George opened his eyes. "Yeah, sure," he said sarcastically.

He was alone. The elevator continued up, stopping at the thirty-first floor and the doors opened. George didn't get off. He pushed the button for thirty-two. The elevator rose one more floor—to the top floor—*her* floor. He straightened his tie as the doors slowly opened.

Grayness. He stepped onto the foyer, a bit unsteady, looking left, then right. The only light was the natural light that slipped from underneath doorways or through glass fronts on the doors that lined a hallway cluttered with silhouettes of scaffolding, ladders, and small generators. All was quiet. George belched, tasting gastric acid. "Yuk!" he hissed, placing a hand on his stomach again.

He took a breath and headed down the hallway. "Hellooo!" he called out.

No response. He tried again, this time a little louder. "Anybody there?"

Nothing.

He recalled that her office was the fourth window from the right corner of the building. He continued down the hallway toward what was the fourth doorway from the end of the hall. These offices faced north, toward the B of A Building. He stepped over and around a nest of thick electrical wires and small hoses that looked like giant boa constrictors while carefully maneuvering past piles of sheetrock and stacks of two-by-fours. Everything was covered in dust.

Nobody's been here for days — maybe weeks.

George stood at the doorway to the office he believed — he knew — was Anne's. No name or title was painted on the door. He listened. Nothing. He looked down to see the natural light coming from beneath the door. It lit the dust-covered toes of what were once his polished shoes. George Thomas Cole inhaled deeply, and exhaled slowly. He reached for the brass doorknob, squeezed and turned it, and, finding it unlocked, pushed the door open.

"Hello! Anne?" he said, sticking his head in. "It's me, George. First Fargo Securities. From across the way."

He stepped inside the dim room and saw that it was totally empty, just as he'd seen it from his own office, minutes earlier. The floor was covered in dust. No footprints. No indications of furniture being removed. No sign of *any* recent occupation.

He walked to the window to see what her view had been like. He was surprised at the distance and the angle to his office, thinking how difficult it would be to see each other clearly.

"What the hell!" he cried out. "What's going on?" He strolled about the office, looking for anything—any clues—to indicate that there had been a beautiful young woman dressed in twenties-style clothes here, placing orders with First Fargo all week.

He found nothing. He took one more look out the window, almost expecting to see her looking down at him from his office. But she wasn't there. *She wasn't anywhere!*

He turned and scanned the room again. "I don't get it. Nobody's been here!" He walked back to the door, took one last look... and closed the door. He stopped and this time placed both his hands on his abdomen. "Uh oh," he whispered. He increased his gait as he headed back toward the elevator.

He pushed the small round button and immediately he heard the cables tense, the motors whirring.

There was a dumpster to his left mostly filled with

pieces of broken sheetrock, the remnants of sawed-off plywood and planks, great clouds of pinkish insulation, torn sheets of what looked like asbestos, shattered glass, and just plain garbage, mostly from local fast-food restaurants and Chinese take-outs.

The elevator 'binged' its arrival. George paused, turned and looked at the dumpster, thinking he might need it. But when the doors slid open, he swung back and hurried into the elevator, pressing **L** for Lobby. The doors closed and the elevator dropped the thirty-two floors without a stop.

George Thomas Cole hustled the best he could across Pine back to his building and up to First Fargo Securities on the thirty-third floor. He nodded to Jessica and, stiffly, controlling himself, power-walked back to his office. There were a half-dozen new messages waiting for him.

He slowly let himself down into his chair and checked the market. It was down only 163 points and continuing to gain strength. Just then, the phone rang. He could see it was David Walker.

"David! Can you believe this market? My apologies that we didn't talk earlier this morning, but I was buried in a fairly serious problem that needed my immediate attention." George tried to get comfortable in his chair.

"I was wondering where you were."

"Probably best that we didn't connect at the opening. We may have overreacted and sold out some of your solid positions. I see most of the blue chips have rallied."

"I agree. I *was* ready to bail."

George, hesitant, asked his friend, "By the way, David, you know our Hydro-Yield Energy? And Land Opportunity Enterprises?"

David thought for a moment. "No. They trade on the New York? Are they something you like?"

"What are you talking about? You own them. We discussed them at lunch yesterday."

"Whoa, friend. You okay? We didn't have lunch yesterday. I'm meeting you this Thursday at Sam's."

"What..." George stopped himself. He looked about his desk, spied the top half of the Sporting Green which had slid partway out of the front section of the *Chronicle*. Big, bold headlines read:

49ERS KICK RAVENS 23 – 21!

Just below, partially covered, was a photo of a football sailing between goalposts.

"What the fuck?" George exclaimed.

"George? What's going on? You sure you're okay?"

George closed his eyes and saw Anne Morrow waving at him from across the way.

"You there?"

"David, I'm not sure what's going on... Look, I better go..."

"Woman involved, I bet." David cut-in, teasingly.

George paused, set the phone down on his desk,

swung around in his chair, facing the window.

"Matter of fact, there *was* a woman involved, David — slim and stylish — a woman of infinite beauty."

"What's that George? I can't hear you. *George*?"

George rose unsteadily. He went to take a step toward the window but stopped. Instead, he turned and cautiously marched out of his office and down the hall toward the restroom. He pushed through the entrance, staggered to the nearest stall, stepped in, and locked the metal door behind him. He spun around, lifted the toilet seat, bent over, and threw up.

HERO JONES

"Sorry, Herm, but we need your office for a new broker we're bringing over from Merrill. Got a nice little place for you along the south side. Just until things pick up for you... And they will. You're a good man, a good broker, Herm. But you know how it is. Look, anything I can do, you let me know." He paused. "We'll have your things moved over by tomorrow morning."

Herman Roosevelt Jones dragged himself out of the slick, leather, guest chair of his manager's corner office and trudged back to his spacious workplace just two doors down. His, for only one more day. His, since First Fargo Securities had moved to 555 California twelve years ago.

Un – fucking – believable!

The south side hallway was known as BITS, where brokers-in-training and brokers-in-trouble 'resided.' Brokers coming, brokers going. It wasn't that he didn't understand his manager's decision. Herm knew the brokerage business, knew it was driven by production. New clients. New assets. There was no standing still. Like the great white shark, you swam forward or you drowned.

At fifty-eight years old, and thirty-two years in the investment business, he had little to show. A failed marriage with its whopping alimony payments had put the hurt on his savings. Fortunately, there had been no kids. He contributed modest amounts to his 40lk, had minimal military benefits, and maintained a checking account to take care of his daily and monthly needs.

He was a good financial advisor, savvy with stocks and bonds, conscientious, and focused. His "book"—his clientele—had been solid through the years. He'd built up his asset base and established loyalty with most of his clients. But like some senior brokers do, Herm had become sedentary. And before long, he'd lost over fifteen percent of his client base to deaths, transfers, and managed programs without replacing them. This amounted to almost twenty-five percent of his annual gross. Add to that the inactivity of many of his customers due to the current market, and Herm had seen his income drop to almost half of what it had been a mere three years before. He wasn't moving forward; he was gasping for air.

Then, there was his mom. She, at eighty-two, suffered from diabetes, had arthritis issues, and was beginning to show signs of Alzheimer's. He knew that she'd soon need someone to care for her full time. And so, just over a year ago, ironically—or conveniently—Herm, who no longer could afford his impressive two-bedroom flat in the Presidio, moved in with his mother. She got the caregiver she needed, and Herm found a place he could afford.

Life with Mom wasn't so bad. She enjoyed her TV soap operas; she knitted... and was hooked on Word Search. Fortunately, she was still able to 'take care' of her personal needs, though dressing herself was not one of her strengths—many 'outfits' were strange blends of plaids and stripes and paisleys. Meanwhile, Herm did the cooking, paid the bills, and made sure Mom took her meds. Most evenings, he listened to his beloved San Francisco Giants on KNBR radio, slowly but surely, realizing that the 2010 World Series Champs would not returning to defend their title. After the games, he'd spend time reading financial reports, taking notes, and working on his computer. Occasionally, usually on the weekends, he and Mom would play dominoes or gin rummy and, most of the time, she'd soundly beat him.

"Why do you let me win, Hero?"

"I don't, Mom," he lied.

Early the next morning, Herman Roosevelt Jones stood in his 'new' office, half-buried by boxes scattered on the floor like headstones. A brisk autumn sun peeked over the Hayward hills and sent a clean, bright light streaking across the Bay and through his window. He immediately lowered the window's huge shade and turned off the overhead fluorescents—an ambiance he preferred.

He slumped into the worn, Naugahyde chair at his desk—a desk so old it had cigarette burns lined up along the edges.

BITS! Who would have thunk? Look at this place. No bigger than a damn cubicle! Not even half of what I had!

He got up and kicked the nearest box. A stock guide and a coffee mug went flying.

"Damn, damn, damn!" he cried, "What has happened to me?"

He picked up the cup, reached for the stock guide and tossed them roughly in the nearest carton while looking about the room. There was no solace to be found anywhere. He collapsed in his chair and covered his face with his hands.

Seems like whatever I do lately, things just get worse.

He looked up. "Damn it, there must be something I can do... somebody who can..."

The phone suddenly rang.

He could see it was from the front desk.

"Jessica. What's up?"

"Hey, Herm. You'll never believe what just happened. An older, Asian man—dressed in a bright orange robe—just appeared at my desk. Funny. I didn't even hear the elevator come up. Anyway, he placed a small box on my desk and said, 'For Mr. Hero Jones.' Before I could get his name, my phone rang and by the time I'd forwarded the call, he was gone! Very strange." She paused. "Are you *Hero* Jones?"

Herm hesitated. "Ah... yeah. Something my

mother… Nevermind. I'll be right over…"

"Okay."

He hung up, leaving his hand on the phone. Nobody called him 'Hero' except his mom. And she'd never send anything to him at the office.

I don't think she even knows where I work.

He walked to the front desk, taking the scenic route to avoid passing by his manager's office.

"Hey, Herm. Here you go." Jessica handed him the small, oddly wrapped box.

"Thanks, Jessica."

"Hey, no problem. So what's with the 'Hero'?"

Just then the bell pinged, announcing the elevator arriving at the thirty-third floor. They both turned and a couple walked out, heading for the front desk.

"Gotta go." Herm backed away, turned, and marched back to his office.

He sat, setting the curious little package before him. It was wrapped in a thin bark and tied with string that looked like straw.

"*Definitely* not from Mom," he whispered.

He slipped off the fragile tie and set it aside. The bark sides fell open, revealing a neatly folded square of bright red rice paper. He slowly unwrapped the smooth crackly tissue and as he did, a coin slipped out, tumbling onto his desk, where it spun round and round before gravity finally brought it to rest. Picking it up and holding it between his index finger and thumb, Herm studied it, saw it wasn't much bigger than a quarter, probably made of bronze and covered in a greenish-blue patina. There was a small square hole in the center. The face décor was a jungle relief with the raised words *Hai Mong* arched at the top, and *Muốn,* in a reverse arch, at the bottom. He turned the coin over and saw that both sides were identical. Then Herm remembered. His eyes grew large, and he dropped the coin on his desk.

God in heaven! It can't be!

He knew of this extraordinary coin. And of the legend of *Hai Mong Muốn!* And he knew what the words meant.

Two Desires.

He couldn't turn his eyes away. The small, round object pulled at him, gripped him.

Images rose of a war long ago in a faraway land. And of a young Vietnamese Cao Dai monk whom he'd pulled from a small monastery engulfed in flames just west of My Tho. The lad's leg had been shattered, his body burned and pierced with shrapnel. Herm recalled attempting to aid the badly wounded young man—could still hear his screams of pain, his pleas for help, his promise of giving Herm some 'magic coin' called the *Hai Mong Muốn. And* Herm remembered the brutal voice of his commanding officer, lieutenant Donlevy. "Let him be! Quit trying to be a *hero,* Jones, or you're gonna need somebody to save *your* fucking ass! Now get your shit. We're outta here!"

Eighteen-year-old Herm discreetly dropped a

canteen of water and a blanket behind and ran to catch up with his platoon. Unknown to Herm, the monk had reached out to him and whispered, "Hero... Jones."

Herman Roosevelt Jones surfaced from his reverie.

This has gotta be some sort of joke.

He picked up the coin, let it lie in the flat of his hand. It issued a warmth, drew him in... he stared, mesmerized.

Jesus... what if... what IF it could grant one's desires? What would I... What wishes would I make?

Herm smiled. His first instinct was to 'wish' a great mishap upon his manager—something like having First Fargo's three top brokers jump ship to Goldman Sachs.

But Herm's more practical side prevailed.

If there were any merit to this fairytale, I'm not going to waste a wish on him.

He thought about the one item he needed most—money!

And how would I get this money? Meet new and wealthy clients? Win the lottery? Hit upon a hot stock? Maybe I'd find a paper bag full of hundred-dollar bills on the MUNI?

Suddenly he laughed right out loud, realizing how stupid he was sounding for carrying on this ridiculous conversation with himself.

Come on, Jones. Get real!

He knew the coin was nothing more than fantasy—a fable. A base piece of metal attached to a fairy tale.

What I need to do is get my butt in gear! Get on the phone, talk with the clients I have... review their portfolios, propose new ideas, ask for referrals, work longer hours, get more creative – and be more aggressive.

Herm tossed the coin back on the desk, deciding the first thing he should do was unpack his boxes. He was halfway through a box when the phone rang again.

"Jones, here."

"Herm? Peter Swartz, here. Hey, Herm, not sure how to say this… I've got some bad news."

"What's up, Pete?" But Herm knew that 'voice.'

"Elaine and I are going to transfer our accounts to Scott Trade. Do our own thing. Now that I'm retired, I'm having a ball managing the accounts and…"

Peter Swartz had been a client for more than seventeen years. Herm had invested his money in solid growth stocks, conservative bonds, large and small cap funds, gold, and some safe ETFs. He'd called the shots as to when to sell, when to hold, and when to add. He'd built Peter's account into a small fortune, actually allowing Peter to retire four years earlier than he'd planned.

"Pete, you sure? We've worked well together over the years…"

"Papers are already in the mail, Herm. Thanks for everything. Hey, you should try this retirement thing. It's not bad!"

"Yeah, sure…"

Herm hung up the phone. *Goddammit! Peter Swartz! One of my biggest clients. WAS one of my biggest clients!*

He sat there taking deep breaths. The coin lay before

him. It seemed to shine now, as if lit by a small spotlight. It called to him. He picked it up again and gazed at those words: *Hai Mong Muốn.*

If only! He sat there, hypnotized. *What the hell? What do I have to lose? If it doesn't happen, it doesn't happen.*

He got up and closed the door to his office, allowing only the filtered light through the shade to permeate the room. Folks passing by would not be able to see him as he positioned himself amid his boxes and faced the window. Eyes wide, Herm held up the coin in the palm of his hand, and spoke out loud.

"I want money! Lots of money. I don't care how, except it must be gained legally. Nothing stolen. Nothing ill-gotten."

Once again, the coin glowed and Herm yanked his hand back as if the coin were red hot. It fell to the floor and rolled into hiding. He stood there, frozen, waiting for something to happen. A minute went by. Two minutes. Five minutes. Herm began to laugh. Softly at first. Then louder. Now hysterical, he fell into his chair, put his head down on his folded arms, and began to weep. Within minutes, his sobbing turned to sleep.

It was about an hour later when the ringing of his phone woke him. He slowly lifted up his head, staring at the phone as if he'd never seen it before. It rang four, five, six times before he finally reached for it.

"Jones, here."

"Herman Jones?"

"Yes."

"This is Kaiser Permanente Hospital. Your mother is Mrs. Lily Jones?"

Herm sat up, focused. "Yes, what's happened?"

"I'm sorry, Mr. Jones but your mother took a bad spill this morning. It appears she suffered a stroke and fell against the brick hearth in her apartment. She's broken her hip, sustained some major head injuries and has fallen into a coma. How soon can you get here?"

Herm jogged down to the corner of Kearny and Geary where he fortunately found MUNI's 38 Geary bus waiting. Within twenty minutes, he was at the Kaiser Hospital alongside his mother. It wasn't pretty. Besides being connected to an IV and a cardiac monitor, she seemed wrapped and attached to every type of traction, bar, pulley, and trapeze device the hospital had.

A voice came from behind. "It doesn't look promising, Mr. Jones. She's sustained and suffered serious injuries." It was Dr. Chou, one of Kaiser's top neurologists. Herm turned and followed the doctor out into the hallway.

"What can we do?"

"To be perfectly honest? Really, nothing. Oh, the bumps and bruises will heal. But the neurological damage is permanent and massive. If she ever comes out of the coma, which we are unsure if she will — she'll be limited to a bed. Most likely, she won't be able to perform even the most menial of tasks. Eating, dressing herself, using the bathroom... you would have to assist her... you do understand what I'm saying, Mr. Jones?"

"Getting well, getting better... is not an option?

"As I said, her brain damage is extensive, mostly to the right hemisphere of the cerebrum. Chances are that she'll have permanent paralysis to the left side of her body and, most likely, her speech would be seriously impaired—muddled at best. Again, this is *if* she comes out of this coma. Basically, Mr. Jones, she will be on life support either way."

"Could I get help for her?"

"She'd need someone—like a professional caregiver—twenty-four hours a day, *seven* days a week. I'm sure Hospice could help. I hear they're very good though they usually help those whose prognosis is a year or less to live. You might qualify. It's a difficult decision, Mr. Jones, I know. Personally, it's my belief that perpetuating loved ones' lives when they're in this irreversible, comatose state, suffering unknown pain and discomfiture is unjustified. Still, it's your call. Take your time."

Herman Roosevelt Jones sat at his mother's side for more than six hours. Then he pulled the plug.

A week later, he returned to his office at First Fargo. Boxes were still strewn about the floor. No one had entered since that fateful day when he'd made his wish—and got the call from the hospital.

He was facing the window when there was a knock on his office door, and Jessica stuck her head in.

"Hey, Herm. You okay? I'm sorry to hear about your mother."

He turned around. It was Jessica. "Hey. Thanks, Jessica. I'm fine. What's up?"

"There's a couple of guys out front. Said they were from a life insurance agency — Liberty? — attempting to locate you. I asked if they were sales reps, and they said they weren't. They look awfully serious, Herm. Should I show 'em in?"

"Liberty? Liberty. Never heard of it." Herm paused. "Sure, what the hell? What else could go wrong? Would you mind bringing them down?"

"Of course not." She looked around his office. "You might want to straighten up your office..."

He looked around and gave her a silly smirk that simply said, *'I just don't care right now.'* She smiled and winked. "You take it easy, Herm. I'll go get your 'guests.'"

"Thanks."

He was pushing boxes against the wall with his feet when Jessica announced "Herm? The gentlemen from Liberty are here."

"Mr. Jones? Mr. Herman Roosevelt Jones?"

Herm turned, forced a smile. "Yes, yes. Come in."

Two men, safely in their forties, wearing Brooks Brothers suits and button-down shirts walked into Herm's office, both gaping at the minor chaos within the office walls of Herman Roosevelt Jones. Jessica followed the men in, carrying a second guest chair so both could sit. She asked if they'd like some coffee, but both politely declined. She nodded to Herm, smiled, turned, and was gone. The two men introduced themselves and sat down in front of Herm's worn desk. For a moment, there was silence.

"So what can I do for you gentlemen? Some problem with a policy I sold?"

"First, Mr. Jones, we're very sorry about your mother. We read about your mom's passing in the obituaries—something our firm makes a habit of doing. Reading obituaries, that is."

"Thank you. But you guys really should look at other parts of the paper. Though I wouldn't recommend the business section. That's probably more depressing then the obits."

Neither man smiled.

Herm continued, now more serious, "Anyway, I hope you're not here seeking any payment or premium. Between the hospital and the burial costs, well, let's say, it's left me a little short."

"Well then, I think we can help. It's because of a policy your mother had with us that we're here."

"Mom didn't have any policies. I went through all her things. I had to liquidate the last of my 401k to pay all the bills."

"Well, Mr. Jones, actually she did. After your father died, your mother received a disbursement from a life policy he'd taken out on himself. She promptly re-invested the money with us. That was in 1963. Our records show you were only eleven. Anyway, it appears she didn't want you to know about it until after she passed away. And, in conjunction with her will, you would only receive the money then. Anyway, over the years, the fund has grown."

"Well, hallelujah! Finally, some good news. I can use a little money to get me through the next few months. That is until I get my business going again." He looked about his office. "Things, aah… are rather slow right now."

The two men looked at each other. Then back at Herm. The second man smiled.

"I don't think you understand, Mr. Jones. Your mom invested in a single-premium variable annuity with the $33,000 she got from your father's life policy. It was a new product for us at the time, and the investment choices were few. For whatever reason, she put it all in a small gold fund. As I said, that was 1963. Gold was about $35 an ounce."

"What? What are you saying?"

"Today, with dividend and interest payments all reinvested, and gold selling for around $1,300 an ounce, the fund is worth around 1.2 million dollars."

The second man chimed in, "And as you are the sole beneficiary, you can arrange to keep the investment by changing the name on the policy. Or you can liquidate the fund and have the proceeds wired to your bank. We have all the papers here, Mr. Jones."

Herm remembered little about his meeting with Liberty Assurance after hearing the words "…over 1.2 million dollars."

He sat, alone now, in his darkened office, reflecting on a monk and a strange coin—and a ridiculous wish made for a lot of money.

Anger flowed through him.

There is no fucking way my wish and mom's accident are connected! No way! It was a coincidence! A Goddamn coincidence! The Hai Mong Muốn coin is just a Vietnamese myth—a fable to amuse children!

Herman Roosevelt Jones spun around in his chair, facing the myriad of boxes before him.

"Wait a minute!" he cried out. "Where's that damn coin? I'll prove it's all a hoax! If it's real, there should be one wish left."

He fell to his knees, his eyes wide and wild, and began crawling among the cartons, running his hands along the carpet in the shadowy light. It wasn't long before he found the round fugitive near the baseboard. He clutched it tightly, lifted himself up, and returned to his desk where he sat, catching his breath. After a few seconds, he slowly opened his fist.

The coin blazed, lighting his face in the dimness of the room. He stared at the image of the Vietnamese jungle and the prophetic words, *Hai Mong Muốn* emblazoned on top and bottom. He smiled an ugly smile as he thought about the possible options.

A pretty girl? Perfect health? More money? Peace on

Earth?

And then it hit him.

He knew exactly what to wish for. Sarcasm dripped with each word as he stood tall and held the coin aloft, "I wish my mother back!"

Nothing happened.

He looked about the room. He glanced at his phone, expecting it to ring. He looked at his door but nobody was there. He waited, each passing minute validating his belief that the coin's power *was* bogus—nothing but a sham.

"See! Nothing! Mom's death was an accident! The *Hai Mong Muốn* coin myth is nothing but bullshit!" he cried.

Herm flung the coin toward the wastebasket and stomped out of his office. He marched past Jessica without a word and pounded the 'down' button a number of times shouting, "Come on! Come on!"

Jessica could only watch.

Once down to the lobby, he left the building and tramped down California to Justin Herman Plaza where he sat on a concrete wall and watched the people stream by. Finding no comfort there, he pushed himself off the wall, yelling, "Bullshit!" to no one in particular. He walked up Market and turned right on Front. At Sacramento, he walked into the Royal Exchange and found a stool at the bar. Herm let out a sigh. The walking had helped. But now, gazing at the liquor bottles stacked across the bar, he was ready for more 'help.'

"Coincidence!" he yelled at the bartender who approached him. The barkeep stopped and looked curiously at Herm, hoping he wasn't already three sheets to the wind. Herm, seeing the young man's expression, just smiled and said, "A double of your Highland Park Scotch."

Once the drink was delivered and Herm was alone, he raised the glass in a toast to himself.

"Hell-of-a-day, Jones!" He downed the Scotch in a single launch. It tasted good.

So what's next for you, Herman Roosevelt Jones? See if your old Presidio apartment is available? Quit First Fargo, manage the money, build it into enough wealth to really enjoy the good life? Or stay at First Fargo, invest in building up your business again? Get your old office back! Show Kevin you're not a loser!

"Bartender! Another double."

He popped the second drink and allowed the alcohol to warm him from within. He took a deep breath, paid the tab, and literally tottered back down Front Street to Market and caught the westbound J Church MUNI.

Ten minutes later, he was climbing up the single flight of stairs to his mother's apartment—*his* apartment—just off Market on Deboce.

"Now, where are my damn keys?" He stopped on the landing halfway up the staircase. "Hey, I know." And he extended his hand upward, pretending to hold out the *Hai Mong Muốn* talisman. "I DESIRE MY KEYS!"

he cried out sarcastically. And he laughed at his little joke.

"Bullshit. Bullshit. Bullshit!" he sang, his eyes moist from the generous intake of the fine Scotch.

He fumbled around, finally finding his key ring at the bottom of his front pants pocket. He staggered up the remaining steps to the first floor where a sconce was out on a nearby wall. He toddled down the dark hallway, the door key now poised in his hand like a small knife as he approached the door to his apartment.

Suddenly, he stopped. He turned his head to hear better. A sound was coming from the apartment. It was the TV.

"What the…" Brow furrowed, he thought for a moment. No, he hadn't even *turned on* his television this morning.

He shoved the key into the lock.

"Hero, that you?"

THE LADY IN THE LARGE FLOPPY HAT

The Rehearsal Dinner

A rehearsal dinner is typically an informal meal after a wedding rehearsal that offers a chance for the bride and the groom to thank all the people who have helped out with the wedding planning. I'm not sure dining at a Trader Vic's would be considered 'informal,' but it certainly didn't stop anyone from attending.

This particular Trader Vic's, located in Emeryville (near Berkeley), is thrust into San Francisco Bay on a jut of land just west of Highway 80. It's easy to find — and a perfect setting for those romantic and special events. Most late afternoons, there are remarkable and expansive views across the bay of the San Francisco skyline where the Bank of America Building rises like a sentinel and the Golden Gate Bridge stands, a scissor-cut silhouette against a Monet sunset.

Couples began arriving around quarter to five (Valet

parking only!), sauntering through the main entrance, down a hallway away from the restaurant, and into a small ballroom where Tahitian décor and an open bar greeted them. Beyond, stood tables for dinner at six.

The sound of soft and wistful South Seas music floated about the room from hidden speakers while tall flutes of marvelous champagne wound their way through the swelling soiree on silver platters held by young men dressed in Polynesian attire. My brother Ben, the groom, and his bride, Catharine, linked arm-in-arm and flashing toothy smiles, strolled casually, confidently, parting the gathering like the Red Sea, thanking family and friends for coming—and helping. Glasses rose, saluting the pair while hugs were shared and laughter filled the hall. All—it appeared—was well.

Meanwhile, in the midst of this near fairytale ambiance, I noticed one young lady in a large floppy hat, spinning around in search of a man with a platter, an empty champagne glass in hand.

"Dammit! Where the hell are those guys?"

I swooped a glass of champagne from a nearby tray and quickly came to her aid, introducing myself and letting her know there was lots more where that came from.

She smiled, her eyes sweeping over me like an infrared body scanner. "You're cute."

Oh boy...

Kimberly White was a waif of a lass, maybe five foot two. And, yes, her eyes were blue. She had a tiny pug nose, bright red lips and a small pointy chin. Her hair was a light caramel in color with blond highlights. (I say this with some reserve as Kimberly never took off her large floppy hat.) But the hair that cascaded out from under that broad bonnet was clearly visible—a swirl of golden-esque curls that rested on her shoulders and down along her bare back. She wore an elegant, very white dress, with a hem that refused to cover her knees. Around her neck, she wore a silver necklace from which hung a silver airplane, suspended by its tail so as to point downward toward a wealth of cleavage that would provide a lengthy landing field *and* a safe haven.

But, according to my brother, Miss White wasn't all cleavage and champagne. No, Kimberly was a bond trader at First Fargo—one of the most stressful jobs on the Street—where decisions must be made quickly and intelligently or revenue—and profits—were lost. Each day was spent scrutinizing spreads, monitoring interest rate swings, controlling inventory, pleasing big clients, developing new business, and keeping her manager at bay. It was not a job for sissies and not for the faint of heart. It was a juggling act that involved millions—even billions—of dollars. And if you were not successful ninety-nine percent of the time, you could be subjected to an enquiry and a possible dismissal. It was a job for those who were cool under pressure, driven to win, and obsessed with the thrill of closing another profitable deal.

Which may explain, in part, why Kim was willing to

take such a chance this day. Oh, I'm sure the champagne helped but whatever the combination, as she surveyed the situation, smiling confidently, she concluded that failure was not a possibility. To her, the whole maneuver seemed a slam-dunk. A **AAA** Muni Bond deal.

She smiled wryly, as she subtly watched the guests over the top of her half-empty glass of champagne, her eyes shifting back and forth. Well into her fourth glass, Kimberly, began planning the operation, believing her campaign was comparable to the classic magic trick known as 'sleight of hand,' where the audience is focused 'here' while you're doing something 'there.'

"Piece of cake," she whispered with a smirk. And now, the right corner of her mouth moved up just a little.

For the moment, the party glowed in fuzzy, alcoholic warmth. Laughter got louder as one drink became two, and two became three. The stock market's recent performance was discussed along with the falling price of oil and the ongoing drought. There were debates over the best venture capital deals. Golf stories were shared — scores were exaggerated, as were handicaps. And, of course, there were murmurs of who was sleeping with whom.

Did I mention that twenty-four bottles — two cases — of champagne were consumed in that hour before dinner by the thirty-plus people in attendance, many of whom did not drink champagne. *Those* folks centered themselves with a foot on the brass rail at the bar and lifted nothing but bar drinks. Some swear that Kimberly White had drunk at least *two* bottles of the sparkly on her own—and she would have consumed more if the South Seas servers hadn't begun ducking her.

But to tell this story properly, I need to digress.

My name is Jason. I'm not only the groom's brother, I'm the best man. FYI, the rehearsal at St. Clement's Church earlier this afternoon had gone well. Ben's groomsmen, mostly my brother's buddies from First Fargo Securities, joked around and shuffled their feet, but they seemed to figure it out. Catharine's maid of honor and her bridesmaids managed to force smiles through their tears and still look gorgeous. I had the rings ready and the exchange of vows had gone smoothly—perfectly, in fact. Both moms bawled. Dads stood tall, hands on their wallets.

The next item on the agenda was to gather at Trader Vic's at five o'clock for cocktails—with dinner served at six.

Most folks know Trader Vic's but because it plays a vital part in our story, I believe a little background is necessary regarding this wonderfully crafted eating place where a bit of Tahiti and the South Seas meet and come alive.

This, is taken from the back of the menu.

"Trader Vic's restaurants combine all things Polynesian with innovation in mixed drinks and unique entrees. Quality in all things Trader Vic's has always been the priority,

whether ingredients, service, or location. Our restaurants have become the standard of fine dining."

Also, Trader Vic's glass and plate ware are of the finest china, boldly — and elegantly — displaying either their famous logo

or some unique — mostly fun-loving — South Seas motif on their mugs, tumblers, dinner plates, salad plates, silverware — just about everything. Here is a sample of an ashtray:

Well, that's my digression. The table is set. Pun intended. Now back to our tale of the rehearsal dinner — and the lady in the large floppy hat.

A few minutes before six, a gong sounded for dinner. A cheer went up, drinks were 'bottomed-up,' and folks — aglow with flush and silly faces — glided over to the tables in front of the dais where the families of the bride and groom were gathering.

I looked down from my spot on the platform at the tables just below. They were now fully occupied with my brother's broker friends and their wives or current squeezes, many of Catharine's friends, and, of course, relatives from both families. There were probably some folks that had wandered in from the restaurant but at this point, no one really cared.

I noticed my 'friend,' the lady with the large floppy hat. Kimberly. She had found a place near the back and was sitting with her boyfriend James Stanton McLaughlin—a senior vice-president at First Fargo. Jim and Kim. Cute.

Jim was one of just a few of my brother's friends I actually knew before this wedding thing. He and my brother had recently become partners, forming BJ Capital Management within the walls of First Fargo. They managed three growth funds of various risks and had done quite well with their alliance, building a substantial book already. Jim reeled in the clients and my brother managed their money. It worked. Life was good for the two of them.

But this isn't their story. Or Jim and Kim's. It's not even a story about my brother and Catharine. This is solely Kimberly's story: the lady in the large floppy hat.

And so...

It wasn't long before plates of food began a steady parade out of the kitchen and for the next forty minutes or so, dinner was consumed while speeches were given. I do recall that the food was good but I don't remember much about the speeches—including my own. *I* do recall I got through with a few laughs and sat down before making a fool of myself. Then, there was the slight embarrassment as my Dad told stories of my brother—and me. But it was heartfelt and received polite laughter and applause. A few of Ben's buddies volunteered tales bordering on the not-so-cool but all-in-all, a good time was being had by all.

Soon, with speeches done, stories and jokes told, desserts consumed, and final 'thanks' declared by Ben and Catharine, folks began to check their watches and, almost simultaneously, started to push away from the tables. There were hugs and handshakes and high fives as they exchanged good-byes. Those of the dais climbed down to join the departing guests. Polite requests and reminders filled the air, ("Let's do lunch at Sam's." "Don't forget golf, next Friday, at the Olympic Club." "We still on for Carmel next weekend?"), as they, now, noisily bustled, *en masse*, toward the only exit, the double door going directly into the hallway that led either to the front door or into the restaurant.

Kimberly, gay, engaging, beaming, was right in the midst of the assemblage. She seemed almost to dance along, radiating from within, thrilled by her brashness, her daring, her audacity as she boldly moved toward those double doors—now just a few steps away.

And then... it happened.

As the tipsy troupe went funneling through those exit doors, merrily chanting the praises of Trader Vic's cuisine, someone accidentally jostled Kimberly. You know *'Jostle.' A verb meaning to push, elbow, bump, or shove.* Some say they saw her mouth open in a big 'O' for a brief moment as she quickly reached to stabilize her floppy hat. It was too late. Two ashtrays slid out from under the wide brim... followed by a bread plate! One couple later said, "No, no. There was more. We saw the two ashtrays, *but* there was also a saltshaker just before the bread plate!"

Why didn't she use her purse, you ask? Kimberly never felt the need, bringing one of those small clutches, not much bigger than a recipe box. She may have gotten the saltshaker in it but then where goes the make-up, the eyelash curler, the lipstick, the money purse, the sunglasses? The Tic Tacs? No, it was always going to be her large floppy hat.

Poor Kimberly! It might not have been so bad if the floor had been carpeted but the floor was hardwood — and unyielding. The Trader Vic's items dropped like bombs, exploding as they hit the floor, the sound reverberating throughout the hall. The large floppy hat had become a cornucopia of Trader Vic's finest tableware.

The frolicking group fell silent as they encircled Kimberly, watching, now, as one last ashtray finally made its appearance, sliding down the back of her dress, crashing to the floor and somehow not breaking.

No one moved. Stunned, they waited for more but nothing else emerged from Kimberly's large floppy hat.

Then, in that sudden quiet, as if deciding it was time to make a run for it, the reluctant peppershaker slipped out from underneath her hat and, in a suicidal double summersault, seemingly in slow motion, hit the ground, shattering spectacularly, performing the *coup de grâce* to her humiliation. She stood alone within the circle of guests, pieces of Trader Vic's signature tableware all around her. She could not have been more embarrassed if she had been stripped naked and found with a large tattoo of SpongeBob Squarepants on her stomach. Tears of mortification ran down poor Kimberly's flush cheeks as she quietly sobbed.

Then something happened that will live forever in the annals of human behavior. Well, certainly, in the history of rehearsal dinners. Catharine's sister, Charlene, stepped forward, reached into her purse and pulled out a small soup bowl with the Trader Vic' motif. She tossed it among the debris in front of Kimberly. A few seconds later, a lady in a white fur took a water glass from her coat pocket, walked up to Kimberly, kneeled down, and gently placed it on top of the growing pile of rubble. One of the groomsmen reached into the inner pocket of his suit coat, revealing a knife, fork, and a spoon embossed with the Trader Vic's logo. He dropped them at Kimberly's feet. Someone carefully lobbed a cup and saucer on the building heap. Everyone was contributing—it looked like one of those rituals where folks partake in a book burning. The room again became a cacophony of shattering tableware. Even

James Stanton McLaughlin stepped forward and somehow, from the back of his pants, removed a dinner plate! Holding it straight out with both hands, he released it, and it quickly became part of the wreckage swelling around Kimberly. Still, no one said anything. They stood, looking down, looking guilty, as if waiting for someone to step forward and reprimand them. Or to explain to them that this was all a joke. Or planned. Or part of the entertainment.

But no one did.

The crowd stood in tableau. Then, one by one, they began looking up, sneaking looks at each other.

And then someone smiled. Someone else started to giggle. A snicker here. Another there. Then somebody broke out in outright-laughter and before long everyone was bent over, hooting and guffawing, until tears poured down their cheeks. Kimberly, at first in shock, also started laughing, her mascara streaking down her cheeks. High fives were slapped. Hugs were being shared again. Kimberly was suddenly surrounded by admirers who wanted to know how she got so many items under her floppy hat with nobody seeing her. She paused, struck a pose, turned her head slightly upward, and coyly said, "Sorry. That's a 'trade' secret." One of the bridesmaids screamed in delight. Others applauded. They loved her! They were just short of lifting her onto their shoulders!

By the time things got cleaned up—and paid for— most folks had wandered out to the front to claim their cars. The valets scurried about, bringing Audis and Beamers and Mercedes to the pick-up area from distant parking spaces. And, as each smiling couple got into their car, they would pause, look back at the main entrance of Trader Vic's and think, *Best damn rehearsal dinner we've ever been to!*

EPILOGUE

None of these stories is true. Nor are the characters real. To paraphrase an expression used at the end of an old television and radio show, *"Any similarities in these stories to real events or real people is purely coincidental."* Still, I'd be the first to admit that the best fiction is rooted in fact, that legend is oft based in truth. And that the difference between reality and make-believe can simply be whatever we want it to be.

– Robert S Murillo

Made in the USA
San Bernardino, CA
17 December 2015